When the Dikes Broke

By Alta Halverson Seymour

Cover illustration by Tanya Glebova
Cover design by Phillip Colhouer
First published in 1958
This unabridged version has updated grammar and spelling.
© 2019 Jenny Phillips
goodandbeautiful.com

Table of Contents

1

The Sea Comes In

"If you could have any wish you wanted in all the world—just one—what would it be?"

Lisa's question broke suddenly into the comfortable silence that had fallen for a moment or two on the little group clustered around the winter fire that stormy Saturday evening. "You first, Dirk!" she said.

But Dirk shook his head, glancing out of the corner of his eye at his father, and Lisa exclaimed in surprise, "Haven't you got a wish, Dirk?"

"Oh, I've got one all right—a big one," he said and hesitated. "Let someone else start."

"Then you, Father," said Lisa. "What would you wish?"

"Well, I don't know—now that I have my new barn. Oh, yes, more acres, more cattle, an extra-big onion crop, maybe a whole new polder rescued from the sea, a—"

"No fair! No fair! Just one wish!" cried Lisa.

"*Ja, ja*, that's only one wish," he protested, laughing. "Just to have the best farm around Kuyfoort."

"I seem to have about everything I'd wish for," Mother said, her face serene in the glow of the fire, and Lisa gave a little sigh of content. There was something so solid and capable about Mother! Wherever she was, one felt safe. "My wish would be just that we could always be as well off and happy as we are tonight. And that's a pretty big wish."

"I think I'll wish for a helicopter," said Klaas, the elder brother, his eyes twinkling, though his voice sounded serious.

"Oh, Klaas, that isn't a real wish," Lisa objected. "You're only teasing because you don't want to tell your real one," she added shrewdly.

"It's a good one," said Klaas stoutly. "There's only one helicopter in Holland. Two might come in handy one of these times. All right, then, but anyway I'd like to see one," he chuckled, yielding to the disappointment in her face. "Let's say a new sailboat—a fine new one. Our old boat's pretty banged up. You and Dirk could have that."

Lisa couldn't help laughing with the others at this generous offer. She was sure Klaas' real wish was for brown-eyed, fun-loving Martje Stuyver, the elder sister of her own special friend Paula. The trouble was, too many of the other farm and village boys had the same wish. And anyway, Martje was away visiting friends at St. Philipsland, where probably other lads were finding her as enchanting as Klaas did.

"Look at Rex," she said, pointing to the shepherd dog, who

had risen from his place near Dirk and was walking uneasily about. "He's probably wishing the wind would die down."

"Rex doesn't like storms," Klaas said. "Not that the rest of us do. Tell us your wish, Dirk."

"Well—I'd like to go to the university and become an engineer," said Dirk, and at the evident surprise of the group, he added defiantly, "the best engineer in the Netherlands!"

"For a boy of fourteen, that's quite a wish," said Uncle Pieter. He had brought his young wife Anna for a weekend visit to the farmhouse. This uncle, not so many years older than Klaas, was a great favorite with the young van Rossems, and Tante Anna, pretty and capable and gay, had won their hearts at once. "It's a good wish, too. Holland needs plenty of engineers if we're going to take more land from the sea."

But Dirk's father shook his head. "Holland needs farmers to take care of the polders we've already taken from the sea. And you are a farm boy, Dirk. Remember that."

"Klaas is the farmer," said Dirk. "I want to be an engineer, Father. Like Uncle Piet says, Holland needs engineers—good ones. It's the engineers who build the dikes that push the sea back so we can have the new polders." He knew, as all Dutch boys did, how much of the country's rich farmland—the polders—had been rescued from the sea by the dikes—how the salt water had been pumped out and the land made fertile. This agelong battle with the sea had always fascinated him. He longed to have a share in it and couldn't see why his father should object.

"And I wish for cotton for my lace caps if I'm to have plenty ready for the market day on our spring trip to Dordrecht," said Grandmother, placidly intervening, as she often did, with a change of subject to prevent a struggle between this father and son who never seemed to understand each other very well.

"You didn't make a wish, Lisa," said Tante Anna, smiling at her. "A lively girl like my Lisa must have many, I know."

"Oh, I do," said Lisa. Her great wish was for a room of her own, however small, instead of her cupboard bed off Mother and Father's room. And to be treated less like a child, now that she was thirteen. But these weren't wishes one could say aloud in front of everybody. She had another wish, too, though she hesitated to mention it because she feared it would make Dirk double up with laughter and Klaas give her his teasing, big-brotherly look. But Uncle Piet, she thought, would understand, and she felt sure Tante Anna would.

"I wish for an adventure—a real adventure," she said, with a slightly self-conscious air. "I've never had even a little one."

As she had feared, the wish was greeted with hearty laughter, especially by her brothers. "You're likely to have one—here on a Kuyfoort farm," scoffed Dirk.

"Well, it needn't be in Kuyfoort," retorted Lisa with spirit. "After all, I'm movable. I'm willing to go where the adventure is." Then, to change the subject, she asked quickly, "What's your wish, Uncle Pieter?"

"I have mine," said her uncle, and he took his wife's hand. "Right here."

"And I," said pretty Tante Anna, pleased but a little embarrassed, "wish for a new good big dish pan."

This very practical wish brought them all down to earth with laughter. Mother stood up, saying with a chuckle, "While you're about it, wish for one big enough to be used for a baby's bathtub too. And now, how about a nightcap of hot chocolate and some of the *koekjes* I baked this morning? Come, Lisa."

"Time for Rex to go to the barn, Dirk," said his father.

Dirk stood up. It was plain that Rex didn't want to leave. He stopped at the door, looking up pleadingly. "I'll have to take him," Dirk said. "Come on, old fellow." But even when Dirk was back and Rex was safe in the barn, they could hear an occasional deep, protesting bark.

"How the wind blows tonight!" said Tante Anna uneasily. "Sounds as if it wants to tear the house up by the roots."

"Don't worry," said Father. "It's a solid brick house with good strong roots."

"The waves were so high this afternoon! Seemed as if they wanted to dash right over the dike," Tante Anna said.

"The dikes have stood against the waves for many long years," her husband assured her, "and there's a dike army of all the able-bodied men around to go into action with sandbags and all sorts of things if there's any danger."

"Sometimes in a bad storm, a little sea water washes over the dikes, but it does no harm," her brother-in-law said. "So good night, and sleep well."

Dirk's thoughts were going round and round over the evening's talk of wishes as he snuggled down between the huge feather puffs in the tiny room that he shared with Klaas.

Klaas was wide awake too. "What a wind!" he said. "Sounds as if it wants to tear not only the house but the whole farm to pieces." He was silent a moment and then asked, "Dirk, did you mean that about being an engineer?"

"Did I mean it? You bet!"

"Father won't like it, Dirk. I don't think he'll help you."

"I'll have to do it myself, then, Klaas. This farm isn't big enough for the three of us anyway, you know that."

"But there's talk of building a new dike farther out. That would mean new polders—new farmland. It's been done before, you know. That's what Father and the others around here are hoping for."

"And that's just what I want to help do, Klaas. It's what I'm going to do." There was a stubborn note in Dirk's voice that his older brother had heard before.

"Well, then, I'll try to help you if I can, but keep still about it for the time being. No need to split the family over it. I know Father wants you to study agriculture."

"You study that, Klaas. That's your meat."

"Studying isn't my meat," said Klaas quietly. "I like to get right into the earth and dig—plant onions and potatoes and sugar beets—take care of the cattle—all that." Klaas, at seventeen, was already a good farmer. "Well," he added in the lighter tone more natural to him, "you can't start being an engineer yet. Fourteen's too young, and anyway, it's too stormy to start walking to the university tonight. So better get some sleep." He gave his brother a friendly clout, which Dirk returned heartily. There was a good-natured chuckle from each, and both boys settled down.

It seemed to Dirk he had scarcely been asleep, but suddenly he was wide awake, sitting up in bed, his heart pounding. The wind was stronger than ever now, screaming around the house, banging shutters, threatening to tear off the very roof. Over the wild shrieking of the wind came the sound of church bells clanging in the night and of sirens wailing.

Dirk clutched his brother by the shoulder, but Klaas was almost too tense to notice it. Those sirens—that terrifying sound he had heard before as a very small boy! "Dirk, it's the air raid sirens. Could it be—surely it couldn't be a war!"

"Klaas! What's that sloshing and splashing? That water— sounds as if it's right inside the house!" Dirk jumped out of bed and gave a gasp of terror. "Klaas, the water's up to my knees."

Klaas was out of bed in one leap. "Grab your clothes, Dirk, and rush upstairs. We've got to wake everybody."

Dirk reached for the switch, but there was no light. Both boys seized clothing they had put ready for the morning and made their way as fast as they could through the surging waters to the narrow stairway.

Even as they climbed, the waters rose too; but halfway up Dirk gave a tremendous sigh of relief and said, "It's dry here."

"And I think I hear Father up," said Klaas.

As they reached the top step, Father came out into the hall, a night lamp in one hand, the other jerking a suspender into place. "Here you are—safe! Oh, I thank God!" he exclaimed. "I hear water down there."

"It's halfway up the stairs," Klaas said.

"Can it be the dike gave way? Mother's awake. Help me wake the others. We must get out to higher land if we can, up by the church and schoolhouse."

The sirens and jangling bells had already awakened everyone, and now they were all crowding into the little hall, clothing hastily jerked on, faces white. Someone outside shouted above the noise of the flood and bells and sirens, "Dike gave way! Get to your attics."

"I'm not going to huddle in any attic," burst out Klaas. "Someone needs to be out there helping."

His father and brother and Uncle Pieter plainly felt the same way, for they all moved quickly toward the stairway. "You womenfolk go to the attic," directed Father. "We'll get the boat and rescue you through the window."

But even as he spoke, water had reached the top of the stair and was swirling over the hall floor. Through the open bedroom doors, the faint light of the lamp showed outlines of furniture overturned, straw mats floating. "We'll all go to the attic—quick!" said Father.

It was cold in the attic, the wind still shrieked, and the rain pounded on the roof, but they were safe and dry for the moment at least.

"It's good I always keep a lantern up here for when I come up for supplies," said Mother. "I think we should light it and hang it in the window. Rescue boats will be getting out, and maybe they will see it."

Lisa, whose heart had been pounding so hard she was afraid everyone could hear it, suddenly felt calmer. That was the way it was about Mother—even up here in the cold attic, with water raging nearly to the roof, she could make you feel safe.

Vrouw van Rossem found the lantern and lighted it, and she looked about at her family. She could see well enough that her young sister-in-law was terrified almost out of her wits and that the men and boys were all but ready to jump out of the window and swim to where they could get help for their womenfolk and others who needed to be rescued, and her good common sense told her that this was the time one member of the family at least must keep an even keel.

So she cast about for anything to say, and as the lantern light fell on strings of onions, bags of potatoes, and a basket or two of apples, she said, "You see we have some supplies, at any rate."

Uncle Pieter looked anxiously at his young wife, and she tried hard to smile at him, but her eyes kept going to the window. Rescue boats must surely soon be out.

"If we had something white to hang out," said Grandmother, "they'd be sure to see that and know it was a signal for help."

Klaas and Dirk dashed downstairs, made their way

through the rising waters to the upturned beds, and struggled back with soaked sheets and a blanket or two. A sheet was quickly hung at the window, and the boys stood there looking out. Over the swirling waters toward the village, they could see lanterns flickering, and now their father stood beside them. "Our new barn," he said, jerking his head toward it. "See it—it's ruined. And the cattle—all gone, I suppose."

"And Rex?" asked Dirk. "Can he get out, do you think?"

Father shook his head. "We can only hope so."

"Thank goodness the sheep are in the old barn up on the old dike," said his wife at his shoulder. "They should be safe, for a time, at least." Well within the new dikes were the old inner dikes, and a third line of still older earthen dikes surrounded some of the polders. On one of them the old barn stood.

Klaas didn't speak. A cold, gray dawn was beginning to break, and now he could see the prow of their own little upended boat poking above the angry waves that dashed against the beech tree at the edge of the canal where it had been tied.

He reached for his pocket. Yes, his knife was there. If he could swim to the tree and cut that line, he believed he could right the boat and bring it under the window. Then, with the help of the sheets he and Dirk had brought, the family could make a rope and slide down into the boat, one by one, and he could get them to safety where that row of lanterns was, over by the schoolhouse. He and Father, Uncle Pieter and Dirk, could then help the dike army or aid with rescues—do something. He couldn't bear this inaction a moment longer.

Klaas usually took time to think things through, but now he saw his way in a flash. Better not talk about it. Someone might stop him. Better just do it. Without a word, he kicked off his shoes and in another moment had dived out of the window and was fighting his way through the angry waters toward the submerged boat.

There was a rush to the window as Klaas leaped out. "Oh, Klaas! Klaas!" cried his mother. Then she doubled her hand and put it tightly against her mouth, hoping that in the storm and wind he had not heard her anguished call. Surely she could not let her seventeen-year-old son show more courage than she did; but, oh, through those terrible waters, could he ever reach that boat?

2

I'll Row With the Oars I Have

Dirk's impulse, as he watched his brother struggling toward the submerged boat, was to leap into the water and swim to his aid. He made a quick move, but his father seemed to know what he meant to do and grasped his shoulder. "No, Dirk," he said firmly. "If anyone goes in, I do."

Uncle Pieter didn't speak, but he was swiftly getting off his shoes when his sister, watchful and intent, exclaimed, "God be thanked! He is there! He has reached it! Oh, my Klaas!"

Dirk longed to be there to help. Four hands were needed, but he could see that Klaas was managing to good purpose with two. He was holding the rope with his left hand while he cut with the other, and Dirk knew his brother always kept his knife sharp. Even so, to the anxious watchers, the work seemed to go slowly. He had the boat free at last, but now Father said, "As to the oars—that is the next question. The good ones, I am afraid, are gone."

Dirk knew that an old pair for emergencies was secured in the bottom of the boat, under the seats, and as Klaas righted the boat, they could all see that he was looking for those oars. He found them, and in another moment he was pulling with all his strength toward that group in the attic window. Into Dirk's mind flashed a well-used Dutch saying, "I'll row with the oars I have." That's what Klaas was doing right now.

The going was easier now, for the strong wind was at his back. He had to struggle to keep from being crashed against the house. Dirk, anxiously watching, made a solemn vow. If he once got into that boat with Klaas, he'd stay there and help, and no one should get him out!

Father and Uncle Pieter were busily tying sheets into a knotted rope, fastening it securely to an upright near the window and keeping an eye meanwhile on the boat's progress.

It took all of Klaas' considerable strength and skill to get near that window. Then he looked up, the tension in his face lessening a little as he saw his father standing with the rope ready. But to his brother's joy, it was Dirk's name he called out.

"Dirk, you're the lightest of the men; you slide down that rope and hold it for the others. We can take two more. Tante Anna, will you be one? Grandmother?"

To the surprise of all of them, Anna said firmly, "I'll stay here with Pieter."

"It is best you take your father. He can help at once on the dike. Then you can come back for us," said Mother. "We are safe enough here for the time being."

Heer van Rossem hesitated a moment, but he knew his

wife was right. All able-bodied men were needed at the dike, right at this moment, and it might take time for Klaas to fight his way back for a second load.

Uncle Pieter hesitated too, looking anxiously at his wife. Then he took both her hands and held them tight. "Anna, I also must go. I must help at the dike," he said. "It is for you and for all."

She drew a long breath, almost like a sob. "Yes, Pieter, I see. Of course, you must go," she said, and she stood on tiptoe to give him a goodbye kiss.

Lisa felt a lump in her throat and a surge of affection and respect for this pretty young aunt who, in spite of her fears, was showing such determined courage. If she can, I can, thought Lisa, and she set her lips in a firm line as she watched the loading of the boat.

Dirk hadn't waited to find out who were the others going. He took hold of the rope and with his eye measured the distance to the boat, trying not to mind the angry waters. If he could throw one end to Klaas and it could be held firmly, everything would be fairly easy. But Klaas had more than he could do to keep the boat steady. There was nothing for it but to take hold of the rope and do his best to reach the boat, trying not to tip it if he was skillful—or lucky—enough to reach it.

Klaas tried to maneuver the boat under the window. Dirk did his best to angle toward it as he jumped out, holding the rope, but the next instant he struck the icy water and went down under the waves. Salt water was in his mouth and eyes, but Klaas' voice calling, "Here. I'm here, Dirk!" guided him, and he struggled toward the boat. Then he felt his brother's outstretched hand, and in another moment, he was pulling himself to safety while Klaas quickly seized the oar again. To his surprise, Klaas said, "Well done, Dirk!"

"Well done!" exclaimed Dirk. "I couldn't have done much worse."

"You could have stood there and been afraid to jump or let go of the rope," said Klaas, and right in the midst of all the trouble, he grinned.

Both boys were drenched and shivering, and the sleety rain didn't help, but they knew nothing could be done about that, and in the tension of the moment, they scarcely thought of their discomfort. The important thing now was to get Father and Uncle Pieter into the boat and then to pull away to the dike where they could help stop that gap.

Dirk didn't see how there could possibly be a break in the great dike that had protected the village for so many years. It was so broad and strong—two or three hundred feet at the base, he'd often heard it said, sloping up to a few feet at the top, where the roadway ran. To be sure, it looked gentle enough on the landward side, where grass, dotted with daisies, grew thickly, and sheep and cattle grazed. But the seaward side was strongly built of stone. The older dikes, which stood some distance in from the new one—they were a different matter, not nearly as strong and well built, but useful as a possible second line of defense.

Dirk longed to get out on the dike, find out exactly what had happened, and help get it fixed, but for the present, at least, he knew he must help with rescue work.

He took one oar so Klaas could help hold the rope. Tall, slim Uncle Pieter slid down first and then helped hold for his much heavier brother-in-law.

The little group watching at the attic window saw the two men take the oars from Klaas' weary arms. "Here are your shoes, Klaas, you'll need them," called his mother, and she threw them to waiting, outstretched hands.

There was a cheerful, "We'll be back soon!" and the women at the window waved in response and stood watching the little boat valiantly fighting its way toward the dike.

"How long do you think it will be before they come back

for us?" Tante Anna asked. Her voice trembled a little.

"Just as soon as they can, I'm sure of that," Mother answered.

The dull early morning light showed the stormy waters rushing inland, covering not only the village but the rich farmland as far as they could see. Not much more than the roof of the new barn Father was so proud of showed above the water now. Their neighbors' houses and barns were all but submerged.

"Look!" exclaimed Grandmother. "The Klupts! Out on the roof! Their attic must be filled with water. It is lower than ours." They looked and saw their nearest neighbors, father and mother and three small children, clinging as well as they could to the red tile roof. "Johan has tied sheets around the chimney, and the children are tied to that. Oh, I hope help comes to them soon!"

In the village, too, there were people on roofs and in attic windows. "The de Boers in their nightclothes, the poor things," said Mother compassionately, "and others, too. No time even to dress."

"And some of the houses have no attics. We're lucky in that," said Grandmother.

"Oh, look!" cried Lisa, pointing to the house of her special friend, Paula Stuyver. "They're climbing out on the roof right now! The Stuyvers are climbing out on the roof! Will we have to, do you think, Mother?"

"I hope not," said her mother soberly, but she was busily tucking apples and potatoes into the pockets of her full skirts, and Grandmother was doing the same. Tante Anna's fashionable city garments had no pockets, but Lisa found room for an apple or two. "We had better eat something now," Mother directed.

They could no longer distinguish their own boat, but now they could see two or three other boats making their way through and over the waves, trying to reach those stranded on roofs. "Oh, oh!" cried Lisa, pointing in sudden terror and covering her face with her hands, but not before she had seen a family swept from a roof by a strong, high wave.

"A boat is going toward them. Pray to God it gets there in time," said Mother, managing somehow to keep her voice steady. She looked straight at her three companions. "If that happens to any of us, we must try to catch hold of a floating piece of timber. Already there are some. Then we cling until rescue comes. Others are doing it now. You can see them."

Everyone knew that a tile roof was a precarious perch. Everyone saw, too, that the steadily rising water had reached a corner of the attic floor near the stairway and was beginning to spread, slowly but surely, toward them.

"Oh, shouldn't they be getting back?" Tante Anna cried, clasping her hands tightly together, her voice shrill with fear. "They ought to be back by now!"

Lisa had been thinking the same thing, and she looked quickly at her mother. "Those old oars—they may have broken," she said in a low voice.

"It is hard to tell what keeps them," said Mother. "One thing is certain; we cannot stay here." For the water was steadily surging upward. "We must get to the roof. Can you make it, Oma?" she asked. Grandmother answered with a firm nod. "And Anna?"

"If Oma can, I surely should be able to," said Tante Anna, who had control of herself again.

"Lisa, I know, can climb like a monkey," said her mother. "Her brothers have seen to that."

"Let me go first," said Lisa sturdily. "I can do it most easily, and I can cling to the dormer window with one hand and lend the other hand to help the rest."

"I go next," said Anna steadily.

"That is right," said her sister-in-law with an approving

nod. "Then Oma. I come last and can help her."

Grandmother, short and plump though she was, got out of the window with more agility than anyone expected. Somehow, each helping the other, they managed it.

Once on the roof, they settled themselves as securely as they could. No one said much as they perched there, the waves just below them, the cold rain pounding down.

"They *must* come soon!" Mother said. "They know the danger."

"They will come," Grandmother said confidently.

But moments that seemed hours and hours that seemed days went by, and still no boat came. Now and then a tile, loosened by the storm, rattled noisily off the roof. Sometimes a wave washed almost to their feet. Looking toward the village, they could see roofs that had once been tenanted, vacant now.

"I thank God that we are built on a small bit of higher ground. That may be our salvation," said Mother.

Tante Anna said nothing. She was using all her energy trying to cling to a corner of the dormer window.

Lisa had climbed to the peak of the roof and sat in silence, watching, watching, as the morning dragged on. She saw people washed off roofs, managing to reach trees and pull themselves up to the doubtful refuge of branches bending in the heavy wind. Others were in the water clinging to boards, buffeted by the high waves but managing somehow to hold fast.

The few rescue boats were working hard, getting people out of the water, out of trees, going to roofs, somehow getting people off and, they all hoped, to safety. But the boats were going to houses that were close together. The van Rossem farmhouse was farther away, and rescue boats must go, they all knew, where they could get the most people with the least difficulty, before they took the more scattered ones.

Paula Stuyver's family had been rescued, all of them. It would be like Paula to try to get someone out to the van Rossems, Lisa knew.

At least they were all managing to hold on. But then came a higher wave. Lisa shut her eyes and held on tight. She heard a half-choked, terrified cry and gave one herself as she opened her eyes and looked. Mother and Oma were still safe, but Tante Anna had lost her hold and been swept away.

From the bottom of her heart, Lisa hoped Tante would remember what Mother had said about catching hold of a timber and hanging on until help came. And she remembered with a little flash of hope that Uncle Pieter had spoken proudly of his wife's swimming skill.

Lisa, a good swimmer herself, longed to go to her aid; but even from her vantage point on the ridge, she could catch no glimpse of her.

Pretty, frightened Tante Anna, trying so hard to be brave, seemed to have disappeared completely. Lisa could hear her mother calling, "Anna! Anna! Anna!" But there was no answer.

3

The Search Begins

"What are we to say to Pieter? Oh, what are we to say to Pieter?" Mother exclaimed. "How can we tell him his Anna was swept away in the flood? Oh, Oma, what can we say when the boat comes back?"

Oma's face, usually so cheerful, was somber now. "It is not only Anna, but also the little one that is on the way."

"Pieter I know expected help to be here long before this. They all did," Mother said, and for the first time there was despair in her voice.

"Mother! Oma!" Lisa cried from her perch on the peak of the roof. "Here they come! Here comes the boat!" But now she saw it was not their boat. This boat was manned by

Paula's brother, Gerrit, and there beside him was Dirk. What could have happened to their own boat? And were the others safe?

There were many questions to be asked and answered, but the first one was, how were they to get into the boat? Gerrit knew the answer to that. The boys brought their boat as near as they dared under the eaves, and Gerrit called out, "You'll have to get to the edge of the roof and jump in. That's what we all did. We'll do our best to keep the boat steady. If you fall into the water, we'll fish you out."

"Can you take us all?" asked Mother doubtfully. "Would it be safe?"

"Safer than to leave you here," said Dirk quickly. "Lisa and Anna are light. Why, isn't Anna here?" he asked, with a sudden sharp intake of breath.

"Anna—was swept off the roof," his mother said huskily. "We pray she is managing to keep afloat. It may be we can find her as we go. It is what I hope."

"Oh, yes!" exclaimed Dirk. "Oh, we must!"

"We'll try, surely," said Gerrit. "Come, then. Lisa first."

Lisa, quick and lithe, reached for his outstretched hand and made the leap without much difficulty.

Oma, looking down at the angry waters, clung to the edge of the dormer window for a moment; then she too set her chin resolutely and jumped. But in spite of helping hands, she went right into the icy water. Her full skirts, billowing out, helped keep her up, and among them, they pulled her into the boat.

Mother, the last on the roof, made the jump safely.

A small boat tossed by high waves was not an easy place in which to talk, but there were things that must be said as they struggled on.

"We'll take you to the schoolhouse. It's dry yet up there on the mound—crowded with women and children, but there's a fire, and Grandmother here, can dry out and maybe have a cup of tea," said Gerrit. "That's where Mother and Paula are."

Welcome as this sounded, they were too anxious about Anna to appreciate it fully. "We'll all keep a sharp watch," said Mother, but no one needed to be told.

Lisa couldn't believe they would not find dear Tante Anna clinging to some floating board, and her quick eyes darted everywhere; but there was no sign of her. "Perhaps she was able to float or swim to some safe place," she said, refusing to give up hope.

"She could be floating farther away than we have come," said Dirk. "These waves can carry you a long way—and fast—if you're going with them instead of fighting them."

"What made you so long in getting back?" his mother asked.

"One of our oars broke on the way over. We managed to find a board at last that would do, and we used it to get to the dike. They are trying to get it into good enough shape to use. Uncle Pieter was fit to be tied, I can tell you."

"All the rescue boats we can muster are needed," said Gerrit. "Men, too. The older men can do more on the dike— handle the sandbags better and quicker for filling in those gaps the waters tore. So Dirk is my partner in the rescue boat."

"Until our own boat is ready, at least," said Dirk.

"I can help Klaas row," volunteered Lisa eagerly. "That would leave you free to help Gerrit."

"We'll see about that later," said Dirk. "Here we are at last."

On a man-made mound at one end of the village stood the old church, with two or three houses clustered around it and the newer schoolhouse. It was here in the schoolhouse that people were gathering.

As the van Rossems went in, they saw the room already crowded with people trying to dry out their wet clothes by the fire, sipping the cups of hot tea some of the women had managed to provide.

For the first few moments, it seemed like a wonderful dream just to be in a warm, dry room, out of the wind and sleet, safe for the time at least and with a solid floor under their feet. It was good to see how quickly and kindly folk made room for Oma by the fire and provided her with a cup of tea.

Faces around them showed both relief and anxiety. Though thankful for some measure of safety themselves, almost everyone was looking for friends or relatives. Some few people who had not been far off and had been roused in time had made their way to the schoolhouse on foot, through the rising waters, but most had been rescued from roofs and attics, a few from trees, and some even from the waves, where they had been clinging to some lifesaving piece of wreckage.

"So you see," Lisa murmured as they listened to the stories, "Tante Anna may yet be saved. Perhaps she is right now being picked up by a rescue boat."

"Let us hope so," returned Mother fervently. "Lisa!" she exclaimed and grasped her daughter's hand tightly. "Here comes Pieter. I have to tell him."

His eyes were darting quickly over the room as he came toward them. "I thank God, here you are! I saw your boat come in. Anna, where is she?" he asked, looking eagerly around.

Lisa couldn't speak, and she saw that Mother couldn't either. There was no need. All the color, all the eager expectancy, drained out of Uncle Pieter's face, leaving it stunned, almost lifeless.

"Pieter, we had to get on the roof. A wave—an extra big

wave came and—but we have not by any means given up hope," said his sister, laying her hand compassionately on his arm.

But Lisa sprang forward and took both his hands in hers. "Uncle Pieter, lots of people were in the water and found boards or something to hang onto. And you know, Tante Anna is a good swimmer."

"The water is so cold—so cold," muttered her uncle. "And she—is not very strong—or very big. I should never have left her. I should have stayed."

"You couldn't do anything but what you did," said his sister vehemently. "You mustn't blame yourself. Even if you'd been on the roof with us, you couldn't have kept the wave from washing her off."

Lisa couldn't bear to see that look on his face, usually so gay and full of fun. She herself had been so vividly picturing Tante Anna's struggle that she knew very well how clearly it all came to him.

"Uncle Piet," she said, looking up at him with earnest blue eyes, "Is our boat ready?"

"I guess so," he said in a dull voice.

Lisa gave his hands a pull as if to jerk him back to activity. "Let's you and me take the boat and go and find her, Uncle Piet," she said urgently. "We can rescue others on the way. I know we'll find her! I know we will! Let's go!"

Uncle Pieter looked down at her and ran his hand through his thick, curly dark hair as if that would help clear his dazed thoughts, and Lisa could see courage and determination taking the place of stunned hopelessness.

"Yes, let's go, Lisa. We'll find her. We'll just keep at it until we do. Right now we'll start."

"Lisa!" burst from her mother, "I cannot let you do that! You are not even dry yet, and to go out into the storm again—I cannot let you go. For a job like that, a man or a boy is needed. That is not something a little girl can do."

Lisa's shoulders drooped, but immediately, she squared them. She herself knew she could do it, and there was no one else at hand. Yet how could she convince Mother?

But she did not have to, for Oma had come up now and stood there, her eyes full of compassion as they rested on Pieter. The look turned to an appraising one as it went to Lisa, and then she said quietly, "Let her go, Daughter. I don't think we can call our Lisa a little girl any longer. She grew up this morning, there on the roof." Her voice was low and very serious, but she patted Lisa on the shoulder and smiled. "And, too, she has a way with a boat, and her eyes are sharp. She will be a good one to help Pieter. You and I will have our work here, Daughter, helping the new ones who come."

If Lisa had ever wanted to hug her wise little grandmother, it was now, and she did give her a quick, hard hug—Mother, too.

Someone had a coat for Lisa, and someone else had a scarf. Paula came up with a steaming cup of tea and put it in Lisa's hand, saying, "Here, have something hot before you start out." And Lisa accepted it all thankfully, if hastily.

"For Pieter, too, we must try to find something dry to put on," said Mother.

"No, no," he said impatiently. "We have no time to wait, and anyway, I'd soon be wet through again. Come, Lisa." He took her hand, and together they made their way through the crowded room and out to the boat.

The wind had lessened a little, but the angry sea was still pouring through the gap in the dike. Uncle Pieter fairly pulled the boat through the water toward what could still be seen of the almost submerged farmhouse.

Boards and timbers from wrecked buildings were floating

all about them, and here and there they saw a raft made of
a few boards holding together. Lisa scanned each one with
eager eyes. But could Tante Anna hold to one of those, beaten
about in waves like this?

The same thought was surely in Uncle Pieter's mind, for
Lisa heard him say, half under his breath, "Could she hold
on—a little thing like my Anna? Yes, I'm sure she could. She's
little, but she's spunky."

Before long Lisa gave a hopeful cry. "Look, Uncle Pieter!
Over there!" Not far away, a woman was clinging to a board,
but when Uncle Pieter managed to reach her, they saw it was
not Anna but Vrouw Klupt, their near neighbor. Lisa held
the oars as Uncle Pieter dragged her into the boat, almost
exhausted but not too exhausted to murmur, "The children!
The children! My man! They were all on the roof."

For just a moment Uncle Pieter forgot his trouble in hers,
and, taking his oars again, he struggled on toward the Klupt
farm.

In spite of her efforts, Vrouw Klupt's eyes kept closing, but
they opened wide when Lisa gave a joyful shout. "There they
are on the roof—your husband and the—" her voice faltered.
"Hendrik and the baby—and—but, oh, yes!" she cried with
relief. "Little Greta is there too. All three! They are all safe!"

If Uncle Pieter found the joyful reunion in the little
boat hard to bear, he didn't show it, but Lisa, once the first
explanations and greetings were over, said, "My aunt—we are
looking for her. Did you see, by any chance—"

Farmer Klupt and his wife exchanged a quick glance. "It
must have been she—a lady, rather small and dark-haired, in
city clothes. She was clinging to some wreckage. Why should
you not find her, just as you found my Greta? Here, let me take
the oars for a while. You have rowed long and to good purpose.
You found my wife for me. Pray God I find yours for you."

"Why couldn't we see her?" Lisa wondered aloud. "From up there on the roof."

"The house could have hidden her easily, and then perhaps the barn. It looked as if she were being washed toward it—or in that direction, at least. We'll row there. It could be she has found refuge there."

But though they rowed around the van Rossem barn, the Klupt barn, and wherever they thought there might be a possibility of finding her, there was no sign of Anna.

"She may have drifted, just as I did," murmured Vrouw Klupt, making an effort to stay awake and help with encouragement, at least, while Lisa did her best to rub some warmth into her icy hands. "We may find her almost anywhere."

"One thing is sure; we must get these little folks and their mother to a dry, warm place," said Uncle Pieter, touched by the anxious kindness of these neighbors who hadn't even mentioned their own need of shelter from the long exposure in their desire to help him.

"I'll row back," said Farmer Klupt. "That will give you rest so you can start out again." With strong arms, he brought his precious cargo to safety, then went himself at once to help the army of men on the dike.

Once again, and yet again, and again, Uncle Pieter and Lisa set out in their rescue boat; but though they found and rescued people in the water and on the roofs, they didn't find the one they were looking and longing for.

"Perhaps someone else will pick her up," Lisa said hopefully. "She may be in the schoolhouse when we get back this time." But Anna was not in any of the boatloads brought to safety that day, and Uncle Pieter's face grew more and more grim and stony with each trip.

"Oh, Mother!" Lisa said despairingly on one of those

heartbreaking visits to the schoolhouse. "Why don't other people come to help us? If we only had help!"

"The radios—the telephone—everything is cut off," said her mother.

Help was certainly needed. The schoolhouse had overflowed into the church and the few houses nearby. Mother and Oma and the other women and girls were doing their best to make new arrivals, worn out with the long strain of cold and exposure, as comfortable as possible. Food supplies in the few houses were generously shared. The potatoes and apples Mother and Oma and Lisa had brought in their pockets were put to good use. A few other people had also had the forethought to bring something with them, and it all went into a large kettle of soup which smelled so delicious that Lisa, coming in toward dusk, suddenly realized how very hungry she was.

"Each one can have only a little," Mother said. Most of it must go to the men working on the dike. Gerrit and Dirk are coming now to carry it out to them."

Lisa gulped her soup hungrily and looked toward her uncle, talking to Dirk and Gerrit. "Now shall we go again?" she asked, but she staggered a little as she took a step or two toward him.

"You are not going out again tonight, my little Lisa," he said. "You've done your share—and much more."

"I could hold the lantern. You'll need it soon," said Lisa, but even as she spoke, she reached out a hand to steady herself.

Mother was beside her now, an arm firmly around her waist. "He's right, Lisa. You must stay here. And how about you, Pieter? You should rest, too."

"I'm going again—as long as there's any light at all, I'm going."

"It's pretty dark right now for rescue work," said Dirk. "But the sea is a little quieter now. I could get that kettle of soup to the dike alone. Then Gerrit could go with you."

"I am going alone this time," said his uncle. "Both of you are needed to get that food to the dike, and you'll need hands to take cups or something."

Lisa scarcely heard these arrangements made. Mother pushed her gently into a corner, and she sank down on the floor, her arm under her head. She was so completely worn out that she fell asleep at once, right there in all the noise and confusion.

Pieter helped the boys put the precious kettle of soup safely in their boat and started off once more on his weary search.

The boys' arms were aching as they pulled toward the gap in the dike where the men were working. Dirk couldn't forget the look of stony determination on his uncle's face and the many sad sights he had seen that day. There weren't nearly enough rescue boats—both boys knew that—not enough food; and what of that little schoolhouse crowded almost to bursting? If only boats would come to take some of those people farther inland! What if the water should rise to the schoolhouse itself? What could they possibly do then?

"Look, Gerrit!" cried Dirk, as they drew near the dike. "Something's happened!"

There was great excitement on the dike, men talking in loud, agitated exclamations, pointing, gesticulating. They presented a strange sight, their heads bound round in many cases with gunny sacks to protect them a little from the icy rain and wind, their feet in gumboots, old shoes, wooden shoes, whatever had been at hand. Since before dawn, Dirk knew, they had been working like that—steadily, stolidly. But nobody was stolid now—everyone was shouting and motioning toward the sea.

"Can't make out a word they say. They all seem to be talking at once," said Gerrit.

"Could it be there's a new break in the dike?" Dirk could hardly voice the words. The boys could see water still pouring through that first gap.

"Sure hope not," said Gerrit fervently. "That would likely mean the schoolhouse, the church, and all would be flooded out."

"Here we are. Mustn't forget the soup, no matter what," said Dirk.

Their faces were tense as they secured the boat and carefully took out the precious kettle. In another moment, they were hurrying as fast as they dared up onto the dike in anxious haste to find out what had happened.

4

Fishing Fleet to the Rescue

Klaas was the first to see the boys struggling up the side of the dike with their precious kettle. As he hurried to help them, they saw that his face, though dirty and very weary, was cheerful, and even before he met them, he greeted them with a wave of the hand.

"What's happened?" cried Dirk. Klaas was always one to look on the best side of things, but it must be more than that to explain the happy look on his face at a time like this.

"Help!" Klaas called back, but this was no call for aid. It was an announcement. "Help is coming! They're almost here—the boats!"

Dirk heard Gerrit give a groan of relief, and he realized

that he himself had done the same thing. "How did they know? Where did they come from?" Eager questions burst from both boys, and before they knew it, they were among the men on the dike, talking as fast as anyone.

Soup was quickly dispensed in the few cups available, and no one seemed to mind the lack of spoons. The men hungrily made away with the small portions and handed the cups back to be refilled and passed along.

"We don't know yet what happened. Someone must have seen our plight and radioed for help," said Klaas. "Probably it would have come sooner if the fishing boats hadn't been tied up and the men gone home over Sunday."

"Sunday!" exclaimed Dirk. "Was this Sunday? Sure didn't seem much like it!"

Three fishing boats had fought their way to anchor in the little harbor now, and men in oilskins were letting down rowboats to plow through the heavy waves to the dike. When they reached it at last, tongues flew faster than ever as rapid explanations were given on both sides.

"We heard the news over the radio this morning and got buses to bring us down to our boats right away," said the skipper of one of the boats, introducing himself as Johann de Graaf. "A fisherman who'd stayed aboard his boat over Sunday radioed the news and said you were in terrible need of help all along here."

"A yacht also saw the flood down in Zeeland and radioed, and there were other messages coming in until we left—and after, I suppose," said another.

"Other help is on the way here to other flooded areas in trucks and private cars and buses—however they can get here. How did it happen, anyway?" Skipper de Graaf asked. "Your dike is well made and strong."

"Storm and wind and the high spring tide altogether sent great, strong waves over the dike—"

"Chewed away like bulldozers at the grass and sod in back—"

"Made holes in the clay—sand streamed away—waves kept battering—"

"All this broke the back of the strong sea wall, so the stones gave way, and the waters rushed in!"

Dirk listened as everybody talked at once, trying to explain. So that was how it happened! And it was a bad flood, not just here but all over these parts.

"The news is being radioed everywhere now," said the skipper. "We came as fast as we could get here. We hope we are not too late."

"No, no! We are thankful from our hearts to see you!" It was Mynheer van der Hoorn, the burgomaster, speaking. "No one could have reached us in time to save all. But if you can get our women and children to safety somewhere inland until we can get our homes fit to live in, that will be much— very, very much!"

The fishermen stood looking through the early dusk out over the red-tiled roofs that showed above the churning waves. Some of the smaller houses, they all knew, were completely submerged. A man spoke up huskily. "It will take a while—to get those houses of yours fit to live in again."

"First we get the dike repaired," said the burgomaster quietly, "then we pump out the water; then we start on the houses."

The men's faces lighted as Skipper de Graaf said, "So we thought. We brought food with us and blankets."

Help had come. They all realized that with great thankfulness—not in time to save the ones lost in the early hours of the flood, but in time to save many other lives, to help many who had managed to struggle to temporary places of safety. Their countrymen had rushed with all speed to their aid. The forlorn feeling of fighting alone was gone.

It was Dirk and Klaas and Gerrit who carried the joyful news to the women and children in the schoolhouse. Fishermen followed in boats loaded with supplies.

"As soon as folks can be fed and can get ready, our boats will start taking them to safety inland where people will share their homes," one of the fishermen said. "The question is, how do you decide which are to go first?"

"That is simple." Dirk and Klaas were proud that it was their mother who spoke up quickly. "It must be the littlest ones and their mothers who go first. We older ones can manage, but the babies and the other small ones need milk and proper food and a place where they are not jammed in like this."

There may have been one or two who disagreed with this sensible plan, but no one spoke until an elderly woman snapped, "That's well enough. But what about the older folks? They're usually taken to safety among the first, I thought." She pushed forward angrily.

"What an idea!" exclaimed Oma, and she actually chuckled. This Vrouw Groot—what right did she have to speak up like that? Almost a newcomer in the village, that's what she was—hadn't lived there over ten years! "If we're tough enough to have lasted through some of the things we've gone through, we're tough enough to wait and help here, and thankful to be needed. I know I am!" After that, no one could object, and indeed, very few wanted to.

There were exclamations of thanks and joy as the fishermen brought in baskets and cartons of food—great loaves of bread, sausages and cheese, cookies, and even some milk for the smallest ones.

"We brought also sacks of dried peas. We could carry plenty of those in small spaces. Also our womenfolk saw to it that there were pigs' knuckles to go with them. And a few other things—staples they thought you'd need most."

"Good! Good!" Vrouw van Rossem had taken capable charge of the cooking, and her eyes shone as the food was unpacked. "We have a fire and a soup pot. With all those peas and the pigs' knuckles and onions, we'll soon have some good pea soup simmering. But first, we'll make sandwiches to send to the men on the dike."

The fishermen were glad to take food to the hungry men, and when that was done, they began the work of rowing young families over to the dike and then to the boats rocking there in the waves. With the best will in the world, the work could not proceed very fast, but it went on steadily. In the meantime, the men on the dike were thankful for the searchlights that the fishing boats turned on to help them in their work.

In the schoolhouse, preparations went briskly forward for as comfortable a night as possible, with the aid of blankets brought by the fishermen. The crowding was eased a little as the rowboats continued to take out loads, but new arrivals were still coming in out of the storm and flood. Some had swirled crazily about for hours in boats without oars, on some kind of improvised raft, or clinging to some frail support in the water.

Mynheer Martens, the headmaster, who had opened the wide folding doors between the schoolrooms that morning to give more space, came in and closed them now. "So you see we provide a private room for you ladies," he said, with a smile. "We have also one for the men and boys. And the third room we have for common use. If the schoolhouse had been planned for such an emergency, it could not be better."

Lisa, who had slept heavily through all the confusion, was slowly awakening. It seemed to her she was coming up from a deep pit, hearing sounds faintly. At first she couldn't imagine where she was, but then she heard her mother say, "But the men and boys—can we get them to come in to sleep? They need it so terribly." And the whole day stood out in her mind in sharp detail.

"They work tonight in shifts," the headmaster answered. "Some will sleep a little. Some will watch and work."

The great question in Lisa's mind was had they found Tante Anna? And as she struggled to her feet, she thought she heard a faint cry for help just outside the door. Perhaps even now Uncle Pieter had come back, worn out from the long tragic day, and was calling them. Perhaps, even, Tante Anna had somehow managed to get there. The others, working busily, had apparently not heard the call, and Lisa went out into the little hall and opened the door. She could hardly believe what she saw in the flicking light, but it sent her running down to the water's edge with a loud shout for help.

It was a wooden washtub that rocked on the waves, and two small children huddled there with frightened faces while a woman, limp with exhaustion, clung to the rim. "I swam. I swam and pushed the children," she gasped.

"Mevrouw Heyl!" cried Lisa, recognizing a neighbor, and reached out to pull her to safety. Others, coming swiftly in answer to Lisa's call, rescued the children and helped get the three to the dry refuge of the warm schoolroom.

"So long we have been on the way—so long," the woman murmured. "I did not know if I could hold on. But the children—I had to get them here."

"Courage like that will beat even the flood," Lisa heard her mother say, as the women busied themselves taking care of the new arrivals. And Lisa took new heart from the words.

"Tante Anna," she murmured to her mother. "Has anything been heard?"

Mother shook her head, but Mevrouw Heyl roused herself to say, "Your brother Pieter's wife—the young lady from the city? I am sure I saw her—holding to something in the water."

"How long ago? This afternoon?" asked Lisa eagerly, hoping that it was after Tante Anna had been seen by the Klupts.

"It is hard to say—the day was so long—I don't know when I spied the washtub there in the attic and started to swim this way with it—my man was from home—I think it was—in the afternoon—"

Her voice trailed away, and she was asleep, but Lisa took fresh hope. If this news was right, that would mean Tante Anna had been seen after the Klupts had seen her. She had managed to hold on for a while longer, then. Maybe she had somehow found safety or been rescued.

Another boatload came in now, brought by Uncle Pieter. There was no use to ask him any questions. His face told the story. Lisa rushed over to him with the news brought by Mevrouw Heyl, and for just a moment hope flickered in his eyes.

"I have rowed—and rowed—and rowed—looking, looking everywhere," he muttered and shook his head. Then he squared his shoulders. "At daylight, I'll start out again. We'll find her." And as if he couldn't bear to speak further about it, he burst out, "I am going to the dike now. It is time I helped there."

On the dike, weary as the workers were, there was no mention of sleep. The boys worked with the men; no one thought of sending them to bed. For that matter, there were no beds to send them to, though Dirk knew that in the schoolhouse his mother and the other women were doing what they could to prepare some degree of comfort for the night.

One fishing boat, crammed from stem to stern, sailed away at last, but some of the fishermen, with rowboats and flashlights, remained to help in rescue work.

Together they worked, aided by the searchlights—farmers

and fishermen, burgomaster and businessmen, men and boys. The headmaster of the school piled sandbags with his pupils. Dirk and Klaas worked silently side by side. And still water poured in through the breach in the dike.

But at last Dirk could see that the gap was almost closed, and it was then that he looked up to find Uncle Pieter close at hand.

"Did you—" he began hopefully, but his uncle shook his head.

"Not yet," he said, his face so bleak that Dirk could think of nothing at all to say.

There was no opportunity, at any rate, for at that moment the voice of Mynheer Joosten, who was in charge of the dike, rang out. "Men! With these last bags, the gap is closed, and we pray it will hold."

"Should we not brace it with more sandbags? The water must not come in again. We must have it secure." That was the burgomaster speaking, and for just a moment Mynheer Joosten hesitated.

Then he said, and there was no ring in his voice this time, "Mynheer, we have used our last sandbag, our last timber. There is not so much as a brick left."

Even as he spoke, a stone pillar, already weakened, began to totter.

To Dirk's amazement, there was a quick movement beside him, and Klaas sprang to throw his weight to hold that pillar in place. Uncle Pieter was first to see what he was attempting, and he rushed to stand beside him. Other men quickly followed and braced their shoulders to hold the wall, Dirk and Gerrit with the others.

Above them, high waves were breaking against the dike, dashing the water down on them as if determined to force that living wall to give way.

The night dragged on and Dirk, drenched with the waves,

was almost too numb with cold even to think. He only knew
Klaas had thought of the one possible way to save the day's
work—to save the dike—and that they must stand there till
help came. And then his eyes, traveling the length of the dike,
saw that some of the sandbags were giving way, that water
was coming through.

And now the wind and the waves together tore through
that painstaking mend in the dike, and once again water
roared in.

There was only one thing for the men to do. They must
reach the top of the dike or be drowned where they stood.
With a wild rush, they reached temporary safety. The men
stood looking with despairing eyes as the stone pillar gave
way.

Dirk looked out over the long angry waves, and his
heart gave a leap of hope. "Look, look! Help is coming!" he
shouted.

There in the eerie shine of the searchlights, they saw a
large boat coming their way—coming so crazily that one of
the men cried out, "Must have a drunken skipper!"

"Hasn't got a skipper at all!" someone else shouted, and
they all realized in swift alarm that he spoke the truth.

For there was not a light on the boat, and as it lurched in
the wind they stood motionless with dread, for wildly as it
came, it was bearing right toward them.

5

The Flying Dutchman

The men and boys huddled on the dike watched in breathless apprehension as the empty boat, its masts now far over to the right, now almost to the water at the left, came rolling and pitching toward them.

They could hear water rushing through the fresh gap in the dike they had worked so hard to repair, and Dirk, glancing down for a moment, could see the gap widening. This ship would finish it.

"We must go! We must go!" someone shouted. "Try at least to get to the schoolhouse."

"We're staying by the dike!" someone else called out.

"I thank God it has not hit the fishing boats! But the

dike—the dike will go! It is impossible to save it now!"

And then, right before their wondering, unbelieving eyes, an almost impossible thing happened. Just when it seemed that the boat would surely strike the weakened dike, it was forced by the wind and waves into the very gap they had made and edged so tightly that it stuck there—more firm and solid than any reinforcement the men could possibly have put there themselves.

A great shout, almost a cheer, went up from the wet and weary workers. Men threw their sodden caps into the air and stamped with joy. Dirk, glancing at Uncle Pieter, saw his face light up and heard him murmur in a wondering, reverent voice, "Miracles do happen!" It was as if fresh courage had come to him and to all of them.

"Let us go now to the schoolhouse," called out the burgomaster. "I know the women have food prepared, and we can take turns to eat and sleep." But every man and boy there seemed determined to be the last to go.

"We could count off by odd and even numbers as we do in school for games," suggested Dirk, and the men, chuckling a little, agreed to this plan.

The schoolhouse was warm and dry, and there was soup in abundance. The women listened in wonder to the story of the boat that had threatened the dike and then saved it, and Dirk found opportunity now to ask the question that had been in his mind, and perhaps everyone's, from the moment it occurred.

"How could a thing like that happen?" he cried out.

"The wind and waves just drew it along in that course," someone said.

"Maybe it was the skipper of the *Flying Dutchman*," another suggested, and the people smiled. Everyone knew the old tale of the ghostly ship that roamed the sea.

"No doubt many boats were torn loose in a storm like this," said the burgomaster, "and who knows where they are and what they are doing? We thank God this one came our way and the wind and waves forced it to our aid instead of our destruction."

The men told stories of the day's events while they ate, and the women in turn told of rescues. After eating, some of the men went back on the dike so that those waiting there could have food and a little rest too. Dirk moved to go back with the others, but now the mothers spoke up firmly. The boys, they said, must not go out again that night, now that the real necessity was over. They must get some sleep—get warmed through and really dried out.

"How about Klaas?" asked Dirk. "He's out there yet."

"Did you see what Klaas did—jumped in and held that pillar?" Father asked proudly. "He has earned the right to decide for himself what he wants to do."

Dirk nodded. That was true enough, he knew. He wished from the bottom of his heart that he could do something to make Father say the same of him, and in that tone.

Once he found there was no hope, and indeed no necessity, of his going out on the dike again that night, Dirk suddenly realized how very welcome sleep would be. Warmed and fed and relaxed at last, he slumped down on the floor beside Gerrit and hardly knew that his mother threw a blanket over three or four of them huddled there before he was sound asleep.

The second fishing boat sailed out, and the work of loading the third went on, but none of the commotion disturbed the sleepers.

It was daylight when Dirk awakened, and the first

welcome thought that flashed into his mind when he realized his whereabouts was that the wind had lost much of its fierceness, and there was no sound of the sleety rain. The long, dreadful storm must be over at last.

The storm was over, and for that everyone was thankful; but they were only now beginning to realize the full extent of it. More rescue boats had come in during the night, bringing food and clothing, and bringing also word of towns and villages and farms flooded throughout Zeeland and South Holland and almost to Rotterdam.

"There's been nothing like it for centuries," someone said. "It's like the flood of 1421."

Dirk, eating a hasty breakfast of bread and cheese, listened in wonder. That was the flood he had learned about in school—St. Elizabeth's flood, which took the lives of untold numbers of people and cattle, which destroyed towns and villages by the score, and acres upon acres of land.

He heard tales now of families washed off roofs, of others still clinging there, waiting, waiting and hoping for help, of people marooned in trees which they had somehow managed to reach, some even held up by telephone wires, of horses and cattle and sheep lost, of dogs who had swum to safety. He wondered anxiously about his own beloved Rex and whether he had managed to get out of the tight new barn Father had been so proud of.

His mother and the other women were busy giving what help they could to new arrivals in desperate need of care after a day and a night of exposure to the cold and rain.

The folding doors had been opened again, and across the big room Dirk saw Lisa in the midst of a group of small, shivering, frightened children, patting and comforting them, getting them into warm, if not very well-fitting, clothes brought by the rescue boats. Lisa had always seemed chiefly interested in fun to Dirk, but now she worked with a kind of gentle deftness that made him proud of her, especially since he felt sure she would far rather be out manning a rescue boat as she had done the day before.

He went around to give her a friendly clap on the shoulder on his way out, and she returned it with a wistful glance. "I'm coming out, too, as soon as I can," she said. "I want to help Uncle Pieter again. He came in and slept—but only for such a little while! Now he's out again in the boat. But these little ones have to be taken care of first."

"Sure," said Dirk, smiling down at the bewildered little faces. "And you're handy with kids. I'll try to let you know how things are."

He went out and stood for a moment or two just looking. The wild waves that had made rowing so difficult had gone down somewhat, but everywhere stretched the grim, gray waters, with debris of all kinds washed about on the surface. He could see the tops of their own house and barn—the lower buildings were all gone from sight. A few windmills stood out a little higher than the other buildings, their great arms creaking as they moved slowly in the wind. They hadn't been used so much of late years since electricity had come in, but perhaps in this emergency they would provide welcome help. It would be a big job to pump out all that water.

Of the busy, neat little village of Kuyfoort, only roofs and top stories of the houses showed above the water. In some of the upper windows, Dirk could see sheets out for signals that help was needed.

But the dike still held, new rescue boats had come in, and—yes, that barge in the harbor had actually brought in sandbags. The men were unloading them now.

Dirk was anxious to help with those sandbags. He was thankful to find a place in a boatload of men bound for the dike.

Uncle Pieter was not there, but Klaas was hard at work passing sandbags along a line of men working to reinforce the dike. "Think maybe you could help best with rescue work, Dirk," he said. "There isn't much more that can be done here until more material comes in—just reinforce with what's available."

"We'll have to have a new dike here, won't we, Klaas?"

"Part of one, anyway; but we'll have to see that this one holds till that can be done. But that's for the future. At least we're better equipped for rescue work than we were yesterday. Some of the boats that came in for evacuees left rowboats for our use."

A sudden noise made Dirk point quickly skyward. "Look, look, Klaas! Airplanes! Helicopters!"

The men on the dike looked up in wonder and then waved their caps and shouted.

Through the grime and weariness on Klaas' face, a grin broke through. "Those are no Flying Dutchmen! We don't have helicopters, Dirk. Do you remember my wish to see a helicopter? Never thought I'd get it so soon."

"Your wish was a joke and mine was serious, but it seems yours has come true, and mine has just got to, too." Dirk broke off, his keen dark eyes watching. "That plane is Dutch all right. But it can't land here."

"Maybe they're just scouting—finding out the extent of the trouble and all that."

"But Klaas, look at that!" One of the helicopters had come very low over the roof of a house where people still clung. Now it lowered a rope. Someone shouted directions. A man tied a rope around a child, and the child was hoisted up. Again the rope went down, and again. When there was no more room in the helicopter itself, people were securely tied to the outside like parcels, and the little ship set off to carry them to safety.

"Boy! Would I like to help with that!" burst out Dirk.

"Maybe you can," said Klaas. "You can at least man a rescue boat."

It was not a helicopter Dirk helped in that day. Those were fully manned, and people watched in wonder as they hovered over tree tops and roofs, gathering up folk who had almost given up hope. Meanwhile, the fishing boats in the harbor worked steadily, loading and taking evacuees to temporary homes offered by kindly householders in Dordrecht and Rotterdam, in Zevenbergen and Hoogvliet and towns and villages all along the way.

But Uncle Pieter could use help—it didn't take very sharp eyes to see that. His face was gray with weariness, though it had not lost its determination. "We're going to find her, Dirk. We're not going to give up," he said resolutely.

There was a lump in Dirk's throat that he couldn't seem to swallow, for he knew his favorite uncle well and could see that he was fighting hard to keep from going down under hopelessness. Together they went where they saw signals for help, alert always for any sign or news of Tante Anna, though as the day went on, they mentioned her name less and less.

From a house with the side ripped out, they rescued an old woman who had managed to keep a baby warm enough so that it had lived through the long, cold vigil. They got Cornelius Broek, one of Dirk's best friends, down from a tree. Cornelius had his dog with him. "He kept me warm. I think he saved my life," the boy said simply, and Dirk's throat ached as he thought of his own dog, imprisoned, he feared, and drowned in the barn.

Many others they helped—from roofs and trees and attic windows. There were some who thought they had seen Pieter's wife, but no one could be sure.

But now, from many directions, more and more help was coming. The most exciting to Dirk were the Dutch commandos who came in with machines that could run on land or churn noisily through the water, going swiftly and surely about their rescue work.

Planes could not land, but they could drop much needed supplies and the welcome word that United States troops and trucks were on the way from German bases—many other troops, too: Dutch, Canadian, Belgian, British, French, and German. From many lands men were coming to help, trucks and jeeps, and boats. Help was coming from as far as Norway in the north, Italy in the south, and America in the west. Everywhere people were hurrying to aid their stricken neighbors.

The burgomaster voiced the thought of many when he said, "We ourselves must of course bear the chief burden. But how heartening to know so many others want to do what they can to lighten it!"

"People are wonderful!" Uncle Pieter said, half under his breath. "But I am afraid it is too late for my Anna and me."

"Uncle Piet, we keep finding folks in all sorts of places," Dirk said urgently. "We're not going to give up."

"No, no, we do not give up!" his uncle said firmly, and he straightened his shoulders. "Come, we must start again, Dirk, my lad."

Many loads they brought to the schoolhouse that day, people of all ages and sometimes family pets—dogs and cats and even a canary. Each time there was fresh news of help on the way, and Dirk felt his heart lifting. But now Uncle Pieter seemed to scarcely hear any news. Without stopping for rest, he worked, and though he insisted that Dirk take time for a meal, he went out alone on that trip.

Dirk knew their boat was bringing in more than any other, but though Uncle Pieter helped with strong, gentle hands to steady folk into the boat, his eyes, watching and intent, scarcely left the water.

It was late afternoon when Dirk, his arms weary and aching with rowing, rested on his oar for a moment and pointed. "I see somebody's dog over there, swimming, and he's going pretty slow. Don't think he can keep going much longer. Let's pick him up."

"Poor fellow," said Uncle Piet. "Yes, if we want to get him in the boat, we'd better hurry."

The dog seemed almost spent, but when they rowed toward him, he turned and swam, more strongly now, in their direction, as if to aid in his own rescue. Then Dirk gave a sudden shout of joy and almost jumped overboard in his excitement. "It's Rex! It's Rex! It's Rex! Here, Rex!"

Dog and boat, with new spurts of speed, made toward each other. Once in the boat, Rex lay down on the floor, thoroughly exhausted, and Dirk bent over him anxiously, petting and talking to him. Both the boy and his uncle were so relieved when at last the big dog stood up and shook himself that neither minded being well showered. "I've been wet so much these last days, I don't even notice it," said Dirk with a great sigh of happiness, and he threw both arms around the dog's neck to give him a hearty hug.

But as Rex stood up, Uncle Pieter's eyes caught sight of something fastened to his collar, and he said, in a voice fairly breathless, "Dirk, what's that on his collar?" Trembling with eagerness, he fumbled at a small, drenched scrap of cloth. "Look, Dirk," he said. "It's Anna's little kerchief—she had it around her neck that night!"

Rex, looking at him with big, anxious eyes, began to bark, and now, rested a little, he made a quick movement to jump overboard.

"No, Rex, no!" cried Dirk, holding him tight. "You're too worn out!"

But Rex continued to bark and struggle. He fixed pleading eyes on Uncle Pieter, who was clutching at the little wet and muddy scrap of silk as if it held all his hopes.

"Let him go, Dirk," he said eagerly. "I think he's trying to tell us something! We'll stay right close. We won't let anything happen to him. We can't! Oh, if he could only talk!"

Rex couldn't talk, but he could do almost as well. Released from Dirk's hold, he sprang quickly overboard and began to swim. He looked back now and then, to make sure they were following him, and gave a quick, sharp bark.

Once or twice he wavered. He started once toward the home farm, once toward the dike. But each time he quickly righted himself and swam on.

"He's taking us to the old windmill on the Broek place!" exclaimed Dirk. "What do you suppose, Uncle Piet? Do you suppose—"

"It could be! It could be that—" Uncle Pieter broke off, as if hardly daring to put his hopes into words.

"Uncle Piet!" jerked out Dirk. "There's a signal— something in that top story window of the windmill. Rex is going right toward it! Oh, Uncle Piet!"

His uncle didn't answer, but Dirk had never known that a boat could fly through the water as theirs did now.

Rex was barking wildly as he reached the windmill, and Uncle Piet didn't wait to tie up the boat before he reached for that window sill and started to pull himself up.

Dirk secured the boat, pulled the spent dog into it, and

followed his uncle with all speed. Now at last here was the rescue of all rescues that they had been longing to make. In another moment he was eagerly scanning the room.

He had felt so sure they would find her that he could hardly believe his own eyes. Uncle Pieter stood there, his shoulders sagging, all the fresh hope drained out of his face. There was no sign of Tante Anna.

6

A Helicopter in Action

"Maybe somebody else found her," said Dirk, unable to bear the look of despair on the face that had been so eager and hopeful only a few moments before. "Here's her signal, you know, in the window," he said and took it down.

"Whether it's her signal or someone else's, who can say?" said Uncle Pieter. "It's just a white handkerchief such as any woman might have. There isn't even an initial on it. Somebody was certainly here, and what's happened to them now, who knows?"

His voice sounded so lifeless that Dirk, thoroughly alarmed, was anxious to get him back to the schoolhouse. Mother would know what to do—would at least see that he got some rest. Uncle Pieter, who had been so hopeful and determined, who had worked so hard to rescue others, must be the one rescued this time—Uncle Pieter and Rex, who looked as beaten as his friends when they came empty-handed into the boat.

Rex made it clear that he did not want to leave that windmill. Even though Dirk held him tightly, he kept barking and trying to jump overboard. Not until they got him into the schoolhouse could they quiet him. Fed and warmed and quietly stroked by his master, he fell asleep at last, Dirk beside him; but even then he growled from time to time and moved his head restlessly as if troubled by a necessary job left undone.

Uncle Pieter, forced by his sister to eat a little, slept at last, slumped down as if he didn't care if he ever woke again, his face very white under the scraggly, dark, two-day growth of beard.

He was still asleep when Dirk, roused by a shake on his shoulder, opened his eyes to see his mother's troubled face bending over him.

"Dirk," she said, her voice low but urgent, "Lisa's missing. She started helping with the rescue boats around noon."

"Hasn't she been back?" asked Dirk, rubbing his eyes in an effort to shake off his drowsiness.

"Yes. She was helping where small children were to be rescued, and she came in twice, but now she's been gone too long. I can't seem to find out who she went with that last time. It's too late, Dirk. It's getting dark. She ought to be back."

Dirk was wide awake now. "I'll start out again," he said and jumped to his feet. "Our boat's right out here."

"No, you've been rowing all day, Dirk. You'd better go to the dike and let your father know—and Klaas. They may have heard something about it—or perhaps they can get lanterns and go out. At least they should know. I think perhaps at least one of them can be spared."

Mother must be more anxious than her steady voice showed, or she would never think of taking a worker from the dike. Dirk knew even better than she did the danger there could be in the growing darkness, with timbers—parts of houses and barns—floating everywhere. Lisa was used to boats, but he himself wouldn't care to be out tonight without a good lantern or a strong flashlight.

Father, too, looked deeply perturbed when Dirk told him his news. "I will set out at once. I can be spared here," he said quickly. "Things are well under control. Indeed, they have been asking for volunteers to go to places where help on the dikes is more needed."

"I could go," said Dirk eagerly. "Is Klaas going?"

"Klaas has already gone—you might know," said his father. His voice held the pride and approval it so often did when he spoke of this steady, hard-working son. "They didn't like to see him go, either. Klaas was one of our best workers and quick to think, too. But they knew he would be useful where the need is greatest." He gave Dirk a keen look. "You're tall and strong, and I noticed you worked well here last night. You go and speak to Mynheer van Hoorn. He'll send you along with the volunteers, I'm sure. I'll take our boat and find Lisa. She's probably back at the schoolhouse by now. I'll stop and see."

Now that the matter of Lisa was in Father's capable hands, Dirk ran eagerly to volunteer his services. He was promptly accepted. "Here is a boat ready to start for the islands, where they are in worse trouble than we," said the burgomaster. "We at least have our dike temporarily mended, and though we must keep reinforcing, we can manage with fewer men. You go then, boy. Help on those dikes."

Dirk took his place with the other men and boys who were going. Nobody talked very much—most of them were weary with the long hours of work and strain and wanted only to drop down wherever they were and sleep as the boat rocked on through the darkness.

Dirk would not have slept so peacefully if he had known of the new anxiety in the schoolhouse that night. Father had seemed so confident that he would speedily find his missing daughter that Dirk had almost dropped the matter from his mind. Father was probably right—Lisa would more than likely be at the schoolhouse when he got there.

But she was not, and though he went out on two long expeditions that night, Paula Stuyver going with him to hold the lantern, they found no sign of Lisa. And to increase their alarm, they discovered that she had gone out alone on the last trip in the afternoon. Mother told them that when they returned.

"She had been helping Heer Klupt. But then he felt he should get back to the dike, and Lisa wanted to make one more trip. He told us about it when he came in to eat a little while ago. She was almost sure she had seen a signal from the van Doren barn. She thought someone might have managed to get up there in the loft. He didn't think it very likely, and he felt he must get over to the dike again, but he knew Lisa was used to boats, and when she said she believed she'd go anyway, he didn't see any real objection. It wasn't a very long trip, and if anyone had been agile enough to get into that loft, he said, they'd be able to scramble down into the boat without much help. So Lisa left him at the dike and went off by herself. He feels terrible about it, but no one can blame him," she said.

"It may be that she found some place to get in where some family needed help," Father said hopefully.

"Yes," said Oma. "You know they've been carrying a little food in those rescue boats."

"Maybe she's on some top floor," Paula Stuyver said. "The

water isn't very wild now, you know. I'm sure she's all right."

Mother nodded, but Paula saw how she pressed her lips close together and swallowed hard. The van Doren barn wasn't very far off. If that was where Lisa had gone, she should have been there and back long ago; they all knew that.

Lisa indeed had never reached the van Doren barn, though she had started toward it when she left Heer Klupt at the dike. She had not felt at all ready to go back to the schoolhouse. There was still so much rescue work to be done, and though outsiders were helping generously, it was the inhabitants of the place who knew the likely places where people might still be marooned.

Most of the afternoon, with short periods to rest and get warm, Lisa had been out on the water, and her quick eyes had caught signals that Heer Klupt did not notice. But she had done no rowing, and she felt fresh and rested. She would easily have time for one more trip before darkness fell.

Her eyes were busy as she rowed, searching for signals, for possible survivors still clinging to timbers. She saw many large boards and even rafts now, for whole sides and roofs had been torn from houses and barns, and many buildings were completely destroyed. Her eyes turned wistfully to their own roofs showing above the water. She wondered how they would ever get things fit to live in again, though she never doubted for a moment that they would.

As she rowed nearer the van Doren barn, she discovered that no signal was there, after all. A piece of white board, caught in the peak near the roof, had fooled her.

But now a most unexpected sound caught her ear—a sound of barking. It sounded—it couldn't be, and yet it certainly did sound like Rex. But where was that barking coming from? She glanced again toward home. Rex had been in the barn, she knew. But no, the sound wasn't coming from there.

Lisa looked eagerly around, eyes and ears intent, and then began to row rapidly. The barking seemed to be coming from the old Broek windmill. It stood on one of the ancient dike mounds, its top room higher than the surrounding buildings. She could see that the water came a little below the window. That top story had not been flooded—at least not much. But how and why Rex could be there, she had no idea. She only knew that he seemed to be stranded and in need of help, and she was thankful from the bottom of her heart that she had taken this last trip. She wished Heer Klupt or Dirk or Uncle Piet or someone had come with her, but it shouldn't be too hard to coax Rex into the boat, in case he was really there.

Rex was there, barking a wild welcome from the window as she brought her boat under it, but there was no persuading him to jump into it. She called to him joyfully, patting the floor at her feet to coax him aboard.

But Rex only stood and barked, running away from the window now and then, and then dashing back to bark again in great distress and excitement.

"Must be someone in there who needs help," murmured Lisa, trying to decide on the best thing to do. If only she had someone with her who could pull himself in through the window while she waited in the boat! From the dog's distress, she was sure someone was in that room—someone who must be in great need of help, if he could not so much as get to the window.

She would just have to get in there herself, but where could she tie the boat? There was a projecting board, but her arms weren't long enough to reach it. She'd just have to hang onto the rope and try to find some place inside.

Lisa fastened the rope around her arm as well as she could, caught hold of the window sill, and pulled herself up onto it, looking eagerly into the room. What she saw made her reach the floor with a bound, forgetting the rope in her excitement.

"Tante! Tante Anna!" she said eagerly, over and over. Tante
Anna looked up at her, but there was no recognition in the
look. "Piet! Piet! Piet!" she kept murmuring, and as Lisa knelt
on the damp floor beside her aunt, she longed desperately
for Uncle Piet, for Father, for Mother or Oma or anyone who
would know what to do. Tante Anna was in desperate need
of help, and quickly. Inexperienced though she was in such
matters, Lisa could see that. And how could she ever manage
to get her into the boat alone? With the thought of the boat
came the realization that the rope was gone. Lisa rushed to
the window and gave almost a groan of despair as she saw the
boat floating off far out of reach.

"Rex!" she half whispered. "You've got to help us! You've
got to swim for help!" Then another thought came swiftly
to her mind. Somehow she'd have to manage some kind of a
message. But how?

For a moment she thought, then flew again to her aunt's
side and gently untied her kerchief and drew it from around
her neck. The wet material was not easy to manage, but Lisa
had it free at last and tied it firmly to the dog's collar. "If
Uncle Piet sees that, he'll know Tante Anna is somewhere
nearby and asking for help. He'll find us—oh, I know he'll
find us!" She drew the dog to the window and pointed out.
"Jump, Rex, jump! You've got to get us help!"

The dog looked at her questioningly as if he half
understood but couldn't be sure, and again she pointed to the
water and said, "Jump, Rex, jump!"

This time she gave him a gentle push, and the dog, with a
half-protesting bark, jumped in.

Lisa's eyes were so full of tears that she could hardly see
the dog's head as he swam away toward home. Would he find
anybody that way, or would anybody find him? She dashed
the tears away impatiently and stood watching for a moment,
then ran back to Tante Anna, who was moving her head
restlessly. Lisa knelt beside her, wishing she had some cold

water, some hot tea, anything to give her. Again she called
her name, but the only response she got was a whispered
"Piet! Piet!"

Fervently as Lisa hoped Rex would manage to get help
to them, she knew it wouldn't do to wait for that. Perhaps
some rescue boat would still be out. She herself had answered
many distress signals. It was her turn now to put a signal
in the window. She looked around quickly, but there was
nothing but a pile of gunny sacks in the corner. They
wouldn't show up enough, especially as the light would soon
be gone. Wait, her handkerchief might do. It was fairly large,
and it was white, and anything white would show best, she
knew from experience.

She managed to fasten it to a hook on the window and
then went back to her aunt, trying to make some sort of bed
for her with gunny sacks.

Thankful with all her heart that she had heard the dog's
barking and had found her aunt, she was yet desperately
anxious. Help was needed at once, and she kept running to
the window to look for it. Her great fear was that darkness
would fall before help came.

But now came a sound that sent her flying to the window
again, and she gave a great shout, leaning far out and waving
both arms wildly. A helicopter hovered there, and someone
in it must have heard Lisa's shout, for it began to whirl slowly
downward. Before long it was hovering near enough to drop
a rope into her outstretched hands. A face appeared over the
side and called something. She could not understand the
words, but it was plain that they were instructions to tie the
rope around her waist.

Lisa shouted in return, pointing inside toward her aunt,
and the face looked as puzzled as hers had. Then there was
a sudden nod, as if in understanding, and to her great relief,
a lad who didn't seem much older than Klaas slid down the

rope and managed to land on the window sill.

His quick eyes took in the situation at once, and his lips pursed in a troubled whistle. Then he shouted to someone in the helicopter, and another rope came down. In a moment he was fastening it very gently, with Lisa's assistance, around Tante Anna. Together they got her to the window, and she was drawn carefully upward into the ship. Then down came the rope again, and first Lisa and then the boy were hoisted up.

Lisa's relief was so great that she just sat there for a moment, feeling as if she would like to burst into singing the Doxology. But then she saw they were headed in entirely the wrong direction. "No, no!" she cried, and she pointed toward the schoolhouse. "Go there! Help is there! Mother's there!"

The boy shook his head in bewilderment and spoke rapid words that Lisa did not understand. She thought he was speaking in English, but she had no idea that he was telling her they were taking Tante Anna where she could get the help she needed, and quickly.

She only knew they were going far from home and that the folks waiting there in the schoolhouse would be so anxious, so anxious.

7

What Will Home Be Like?

There was nothing Lisa could do now, so she sat in anxious silence as the helicopter whirled down onward. And yet she couldn't help being excited. Here she was, Lisa van Rossem, a quiet little farm girl, actually flying through the air, and without even knowing where she was going. Once or twice she glanced downward, and before long she could see they had left the water behind them. How wonderful it was to see dry land again!

Presently, they began to descend, and very soon Lisa found herself in a building that looked like a warehouse, only it was filled with cots now and a few tables and benches.

Many were asleep on the cots; others were eating at

the tables. There were women at work here just as in the
schoolhouse at home—cooking, serving, tending children,
caring for people who were brought in. There were nurses,
too, in white uniforms with red crosses on their headgear.

Tante Anna was taken away at once to another room.
When Lisa tried to follow, a nurse barred her way, saying
something very gently in a language she did not understand.
To her great relief, one of her own countrywomen came up
and put an arm around her and said, "They will take good
care of her, my child. They have come from everywhere to
help us. These are American nurses who were in Germany.
Truckloads of help have come from those American bases.
They were among the first to our rescue. And now we'll feed
you and let you sleep. Later you shall see—is it your sister?"

"My aunt," said Lisa. Here was someone who understood
her language, and yet Lisa found it difficult to speak at all.
Her relief at finding help for her aunt was mixed with anxiety
and weariness and concern for the folks at home.

"You have had a hard time, my child," said the woman, so
kindly that Lisa could hardly keep from bursting into tears,
after the long time of strain. But she was determined not to
do anything of that kind, and she managed to steady herself,
though her lip quivered.

"It isn't that," she said. "Others have had a much worse
time than I have. But my aunt—she's so—so dear. Will she—
will she be all right, do you think? She was lost, and I was
lucky enough to find her, and if only I could let my uncle
know! He was searching and searching! And my folks—
they won't know what's become of me either. They'll be so
worried!"

The woman looked at her compassionately. "Your folks—
they are safe?" And when Lisa nodded, she went on, "In
Holland there are many worried hearts tonight. You know

your folks are safe, and they must trust that you are. Where is your home?"

"Kuyfoort. Is it far? We flew so fast," said Lisa in a small voice.

"Kuyfoort is a good distance, and communications are broken, as you know. It is not yet possible to get messages through. Come, now. I can see you need food and rest."

And with that Lisa had to be content, though as she drifted off to sleep, she was still trying with all her might to think of some way to get word home. She was deeply concerned about her mother and even more about Uncle Pieter. If only there were some way of letting him know! How wonderful it would be if one of those helicopters, flying on its errand of mercy, could take her and Tante Anna back to Kuyfoort! But she knew that her family might be evacuated from the home village long before Tante Anna could make such a journey, and her thoughts were still going round and round when she fell asleep at last.

***

In the schoolhouse at Kuyfoort, Vrouw van Rossem waited and hoped while her brother Pieter slept on, his head resting against Rex. Heer van Rossem came in from the last trip of the night to shake his head and say, "But Lisa, I am sure, has been picked up or has taken refuge somewhere." He didn't tell his wife that Lisa's boat had been found, drifting. Time enough for that tomorrow. By then they might have word of Lisa—Anna too, he hoped.

Dirk, on the sailboat with the other volunteers, had no idea that his sister was still missing. He slept soundly through the night and woke to find that they had dropped anchor in a harbor that looked even more forlorn than Kuyfoort, for here the gaps in the dike still stretched wide, and water still poured through.

There was plenty to be done. In mud and ooze they worked. Barges brought in sand and clay, reeds and brush, and bags and bricks. Huge American bombers dropped loads of material to help close the gaps.

Dirk gained increased respect for the engineers who had built these dikes and also for the sea which had battered its way through. Still better dikes must be built in the future, and Dirk felt a great urge to help. This work of filling and carrying sandbags was a long way from engineering, but at least it was helping. Also it was building up his muscles for soccer, he thought, flexing his shoulders as he stopped to rest. But what he really wanted—more than ever, now that he saw the great need—was to have a hand in the planning.

This determination was strengthened by a conversation he had there on the dike one afternoon with a lady who seemed much interested in the work. He didn't know at first who she was, but he felt sure she was a very great person, and as she came to stand beside him in her muddy gum boots, a scarf tied around her head, he pulled off his cap and returned her greeting with respect.

"I see you are piling the sandbags in a horseshoe shape," she said, with a keen glance at the work he was doing. "Can you tell me why you are doing that?"

"Well, you see, ma'am, we build a temporary horseshoe mend around a break. That protects it so the men can do a real mend. And it's the best shape to stand up against the currents."

She nodded and smiled at him. "I see you understand what you are doing," she said in a friendly, encouraging voice. "You are the stuff of which engineers are made for the Netherlands." And with another smile and nod, she plunged on through the mud in her gum boots, leaving Dirk in a glow of pleasure.

A man who came up a moment later asked curiously, "Do you know who you were talking to?"

Dirk shook his head. "I only know she was a wonderful woman," he said, gazing after her.

"You're right about that. She's the Queen!"

Dirk drew a deep breath. "The Queen! Of course! In the babushka and gum boots, I didn't recognize her, though I felt all the time I'd seen her face before."

"She's everywhere in those gum boots and babushka, seeing what's needed and helping folks—the Queen's mother too. When the Queen's car got stuck in the mud, she said to the chauffeur, 'Let's all get out and push.' And she did. With a Queen like that, we'll win through."

"You bet!" said Dirk.

Two or three times after that, he caught sight of the Queen, and each time it made him feel like working harder.

Wherever men and boys were needed most, the volunteers were sent. Dirk longed to get word from home and longed to let the folks know what he was doing and seeing, but there were no regular communications yet, though someone coming from Kuyfoort did tell him that his parents and grandmother had been evacuated inland—among the last to go. Dirk was sure they would also be among the very first to return.

Sometimes the volunteers had a choice of places to go, in case they might have friends or relatives in some of the towns and villages needing help. Dirk, hearing St. Philipsland mentioned, quickly made up his mind to go there. That was where Martje Stuyver was visiting at the time of the flood, and if he could get word of Martje and somehow reach Klaas with it, he knew it would mean a great deal to his brother. So to St. Philipsland, at the first opportunity, he went.

As he worked on the dike there, he asked questions of many St. Philipslanders, but no one seemed to know of Martje Stuyver, and Dirk did not know the name of the people she was visiting. He was beginning to wish he had asked for a place nearer home. It seemed long since he had seen any of the folks, and it suddenly came over him that the van Rossem family was so scattered that he wondered if they would ever all get together again.

His heart was heavy, and when the dikemaster clapped him on the shoulder and said, "Something's going on up there at the store, boy. Want to go and see what it is? Tell me about it if it's something I ought to know," Dirk was glad to stop the tedious work of filling sandbags and go on the errand.

A good part of the town was under water, and Dirk knew that the town hall had been destroyed and that the burgomaster had set up shop temporarily in a little grocery store that was high enough to be fairly dry. Town business of many kinds was transacted there. Permits were issued for people to go into their houses and get things they needed most, since careful watch was kept that no pilfering should go on now that at least the top story of some of the houses could be entered again. And though the dike was not yet closed, planning was already under way for putting everything in order again. The temporary store-office was a busy place.

But today's business was something unusual; Dirk could see that at once. The little store was crowded. The burgomaster stood behind the counter. In front of it stood a young couple. And to Dirk's astonished ears came the words of the marriage ceremony. Suddenly his heart lightened. Here were folks going right on with their plans as if nothing had happened. They weren't even going to let a flood interfere with their wedding.

His eyes wandered over the little crowd, and then he almost gave a whoop of joy. That was certainly Martje standing there half hidden behind some others, though her rumpled hair and wrinkled dress didn't seem much like the fastidious Martje. And yet there was a kind of happiness in her face that made her, he thought, prettier than ever as she looked up at a companion.

Dirk wasn't sure he liked that. How would Klaas feel? And then, as someone in the crowd moved, he saw that it was Klaas there beside her, and on his face was that same shining look.

The ceremony was over now. People surged forward to wish the newly married pair happiness, and Dirk managed to get through the little crowd. "Martje! Klaas! How did you get here, Klaas, and when?"

"Just got here today. I asked to come," said Klaas in his straightforward way. He reached out and clapped his brother on the shoulder with one hand, but his other held firmly to Martje's. "I was anxious about this girl here, and I find she was anxious about me, too."

The two smiled at each other, and Dirk could see that for the moment he was completely forgotten. But then Klaas asked, "And how about you?"

"I also asked to come, and I tried to find Martje, but I couldn't," said Dirk.

"Klaas knew where to look," Martje said. "And I thought he'd come," she added softly. "I kept watching for him."

"She'd had a little news of us from people who came from Kuyfoort and nearby places," said Klaas.

"Yes, I knew how Klaas jumped in nearly up to his neck to take the place of a sandbag," said Martje, her eyes shining as she smiled up at him.

"That was nothing," said Klaas, red and embarrassed and also greatly pleased. "They did the same thing in Colijnsplaat too, I hear, and probably other places. It was the only thing to do. Martje's been helping here, just like her folks and our folks in Kuyfoort, Dirk. We'll try to get her home, soon as we can."

"Klaas, I wish I could go where they are really building dikes. Not just temporary repairs like we've been helping with—really building," said Dirk.

Klaas looked at his brother thoughtfully. That was a natural wish for Dirk, he knew. "I don't think there'll be much trouble about that," he said. "Probably be plenty of places they'll be doing it as soon as the water's shallower. And they'll need help, too. Just wait and work for a bit here and see."

Dirk's homesickness was greatly eased by his brother's presence. Though both boys were anxious about the rest of the family, they could talk things over and ask for news. Klaas and Martje were so happy together that Dirk couldn't help sharing some of the happiness. Even in the midst of the work they were doing now, hopeful plans for the future kept coming through.

"It'll be a long time, Martje," Dirk heard Klaas say. "All this flood stuff has to be cleared up, and we have to get our home places in order. It may be years, but then—" he drew a deep breath, "then we can start toward a home of our own."

"We'll wait and work," said Martje, and added with laughing eyes, "even if we had to be married in a grocery store."

The busy days went by, with some happy times too. Now people began to tell funny stories of rescues—of the old man on a roof who took the rope a helicopter pilot dropped to him and anchored it firmly to the chimney, sure that the strange craft was in trouble, of the difficulty they had in convincing him the rope was there for his rescue. There were stories of great courage, too, of people who had swum long distances to safety, of others who had kept small children alive by holding them very close and somehow clinging to roofs for days until rescue came.

Dirk was proud of his countrymen. He was even more proud when he had his wish at last to see a new section of dike going in. He and Klaas had been moved to another town, and now the two stood side by side on a barge loaded with rocks, ready to throw them in when the time came. Dirk looked with wondering eyes as an enormous mattress made of reeds and brush was slowly towed out from shore to be lowered to the sandy bed of the sea.

"Great guns! That must be at least two or three hundred feet across!" he exclaimed, and joined the greatest joy in the exciting work of picking up rocks and throwing them down to sink the great mattress.

"Careful there, boy," warned a man next to him. "The trick is to get that mattress covered evenly, or it'll tip and the rocks will fall off."

Dirk could see that the men threw the rocks with great care and skill. He and Klaas tried to do the same, and soon they were throwing with the best of them.

"That mattress and the rocks will keep the sandy bottom from shifting," said the man who had warned Dirk to be careful.

"Oh, I wish I could see the whole thing done," said Dirk, so fervently that the man couldn't help laughing, though he approved of Dirk's eager interest.

"That takes time. First, a couple of walls of clay have to be built—they'll be dumped by that crane over there. When they harden, a dredge will pump sand from the bottom of the sea and dump it between the two walls. Then when the water drains away, the sand will build up between the two hard clay walls. More mattresses are put against the sides to protect them, then crushed brick on top and stone in the front, and sod on the back. It's the age-old way the Dutch build dikes."

Dirk longed to see the whole process, to get his hands on the steam shovels, bulldozers, and cranes brought in to aid in the work—at least to watch the men expertly handling the big machines.

But now people were beginning to say the emergency had been declared over. Though it would be many weeks before most people would be back in their homes and many months before the gaps in the dikes would all be closed, at Kuyfoort the dike repair was holding. Word came that the work of pumping out the water was well underway there. Klaas felt that he and Dirk might be more useful now at home and that they should take their first opportunity to get there.

They were both hopeful and apprehensive when they set out at last for Kuyfoort. Martje had left St. Philipsland some time before they did, and though they were not quite sure where she would be taken, they knew she would be safe. She might even be home ahead of them.

"I wonder if any of our folks will be there," Dirk said anxiously. "I wonder where they are, Klaas, and what home will be like, if the water's pumped out."

Klaas was thinking of that, too. But far more than that, he was wondering if, when the water was pumped out, any sign had been found of Tante Anna.

8

Kuyfoort Shovels Out

It was a strange feeling the boys had as they sailed into the little harbor at Kuyfoort and stood once more on the dike. When they had gone away, water had covered the village almost to where they were standing. Now electric pumps were hard at work, and the long arms of old windmills, many of them out of use for years, flailed the air, creaking rhythmically.

Below lay the little town, with farms stretching beyond, and now that the water was nearly gone, the boys could begin to see the damage they had before only imagined. Mud and ooze covered everything—streets, trees, bushes, and houses. Some buildings had been destroyed, others greatly damaged.

Windows were broken, roofs sagging, doors hanging askew.

For a moment neither boy could speak. Then Dirk said, in a low voice, "Doesn't look much like Kuyfoort!"

"Not now. But just wait! There's a lot of work to do, but we'll do it."

Dirk nodded. "Let's get going," was all he said.

As they slid and clambered down the side of the dike and waded along the village street, they were glad of the rubber boots that had been supplied them. "Look, they're beginning already!" Dirk exclaimed. For in the village square women were at work, doing their best to clean it with heavy brooms. The houses they passed were not yet fit to live in, but in some of them people were beginning the work of cleaning, shoveling out mud, and scraping down walls. Here was a house with its porch torn off. In front of another, a large rowboat with an outboard motor stood stranded in the mud, drawn up neatly to the curb like a parked car.

"The doctor's house had the side ripped clear out!" exclaimed Klaas, and they stopped a moment at the sight of beds and tables and chairs in a sodden mass, a large stove half pushed through a wall. Both boys tried to walk on faster, anxious yet half afraid to see what their own home would be like.

Silt covered the fields, Klaas noticed that at once, and a lake stretched between the mud-caked house and farm buildings. Fences were broken and twisted, gate posts leaning crazily aslant. But Dirk noticed something else, too. "Look, Klaas! Mother's home, I know that," he said eagerly. "See how the upstairs windows shine! No mud!"

The boys broke into a run in spite of the thick, sticky mud. They pushed open the door with a shout. "Mother! Oma! Lisa! We're home! We're home!"

Water and mud still stood inches deep in the downstairs

rooms, but Mother was at the top of the stairs, holding out her arms and smiling as they raced up. "I thought you'd be here soon. So we managed to get back, and here we stay! They say it is not yet fit to live in—our house—but we are sleeping at the schoolhouse, and we will soon have things cleaned up." She nodded with such determination that for a moment the boys forgot the dank smell in the rooms and the mud everywhere.

"Where is everyone? You were away, we heard, but you didn't stay long," said Klaas.

"They took us for a while to Zevenbergen, and people there were more than kind and wanted us to stay longer. But—" Mother broke off, and such a look of sadness crossed her face that the boys wondered anxiously about the rest of the family.

Before they could ask, Oma came beaming in to greet them, a scrubbing brush in one hand, the other trying to pull her cap straight. There was the sound of excited barking from the barn, and in another moment Rex shot up the stairs into the room, rushing up to the boys and round and round them, barking a frantic welcome, while they in turn hugged and patted him in a joyful reunion. Next Father, hearing the noise, splashed his way in from the barn. But there was no sign of Lisa.

"Now we are here—five," said Oma.

"But we should be eight," said Mother in a low voice.

"Where are they?" asked Klaas, sounding as if he hardly dared to ask.

"Pieter went with some of the rescue crews. I know he hoped—" She paused again, but they all knew well enough what Uncle Pieter hoped.

"But Lisa—where's Lisa?" burst out Dirk.

"Lisa—didn't come back that day," said Mother, and her

voice trembled. "She never came back."

"But one thing," said Father, "neither Anna nor Lisa has been found among any of the wreckage." He stopped for a moment. "Others have," he said huskily.

"But many will be found safe who we think now are lost," said Oma. "Lisa will be back—I feel it in my bones. And what of Martje? Did you get any word of her?"

"We found Martje," Dirk said, with a quick glance at his brother. "She practically didn't see me because she didn't have eyes for anyone but Klaas."

"We don't know where she is now, though," said Klaas anxiously. "I hoped she'd be home."

"Not many are home yet. But Martje may be in a nearby village," said Mother. "And every day they come. How was it that you boys could come?"

"Machinery of all kinds and experienced men were moving in," answered Klaas. "We thought we were more needed here."

"Boy, would I like to get my hands on some of that machinery!" exclaimed Dirk. "It's wonderful the way they go at that rebuilding! Well, I had a little part in it, anyway."

"Here there's work for all hands too," said Father. "Maybe rebuilding land isn't as exciting as building dikes, but it's just as necessary, and it's going to be a big job."

"How about the cattle?" asked Klaas, feeling that they might as well have the whole story. "What of them?"

"Drowned," his father replied. "Horses, too. Rex was the only one to get out. The window in the peak was blown open—that must have been how he escaped."

"But the sheep were safe," said Mother. "We found them huddled in the old barn."

"Good thing for us we had that old barn on the old dike around the polder," Father said. "I'd intended to tear it down, but it saved the sheep this time, and one of the horses—young Dapple. He did me a favor by being so hard for the others to get along with that I put him up there temporarily. He's not a steady worker like the others, but he's a good deal better than nothing."

"And the wagons and plow and machinery—how about them?" Klaas asked.

"All covered with salt and silt, but I think we can clean them up for some use; at least I hope so. But how we can plant the fields, I don't know. I hardly know where to start."

"Silt and salt all over the house too," said Mother, her eyes traveling over the mud-caked walls and furniture, the soaked rugs and bedding.

Klaas and Dirk stood silent. Then Dirk said suddenly, "Mother, I saw the Queen. She was right there, encouraging everybody, and she talked to me. She had on rubber boots and a babushka, and at first I didn't know who she was."

"The Queen!" exclaimed his mother. "You saw the Queen?"

"Yes, she stood and watched me working a minute and then asked why we laid the sandbags the way we did, and I did my best to explain." He hesitated a moment. "And she told me I'd make a good engineer. And, Mother, I saw her look at a house with the front ripped off. There was a little bed hanging half out of the bedroom. Nobody had been back to try to clean or salvage anything. The Queen stood and looked at it and didn't say a word, and then she put her head down, and, Mother, I think she was crying. But right after that, she waded out into the water and with her own hands placed a sandbag and talked to the men."

The little story seemed to put new heart into all of them. Mother's voice was steady as she said, "I hear the Queen was the first to give clothing of her own and the Princesses'. She has set us all an example of courage and industry. And I will tell you that we do have hope that Anna and Lisa are safe but have not been able to get word to us. There are many rescue centers, as you know."

"Of course they could not get word to us at Zevenbergen," said Oma. "They would not know where we were."

"No, that is why we were impatient to get back to Kuyfoort," said Mother, "and also for you boys. And here we stay, though we cannot get a permit yet to live in our house. But we clean—and wait."

"It must first be inspected and found safe as to structure," said Father, "and it must dry out more. But I am sure it is sound, and the permit will come soon, we hope."

"I have here a good scrubbing brush, anyway," said Oma, with brisk satisfaction. "Among the supplies that came to help us, someone was smart enough to put cleaning things."

"And in a big box from America, some scouring powder actually called 'Dutch Cleanser,'" said Mother, "with a picture of a woman in wooden shoes running around after dirt with a stick. I wish I had her here to help right now. I'd give her plenty to do." They all laughed.

"We'll make it," Father said. "I don't quite know how, but we'll make it."

"I know something we can make right now," said Mother cheerfully. "We have a little fire in the bedroom stove to help dry things out and heat water for cleaning. We can make some tea. And we have also a loaf of bread."

"Sounds like a regular feast," said Klaas, with his familiar grin.

And it seemed like a feast to the five, perched in odd places but sitting down together to eat for the first time in weeks. And though they thought longingly of the absent ones, they were hopeful, too.

It was Oma who put the thought into words. "Every day we hear of families who were scattered being brought together once more," she said. "Pieter, I am sure, will find them soon. He is not one who gives up."

"He is looking for Tante Anna," said Dirk. "But what of Lisa?"

"He will look for both," said Mother. "Lisa, too, is dear to him."

* * *

Pieter had indeed been looking for both. For many days he had searched, going to rescue centers, information centers, wherever he hoped he might find word.

His boat, fitted now with an outboard motor, went constantly from place to place, and as he sought news for himself, he brought many other families together. Sometimes he joined other rescue parties, working wherever he could be of most use.

One heartbreaking day he went to the little apartment in Middelharnis where he and Anna had set up housekeeping. The forlorn hope had come to him that perhaps she had somehow managed to get word through to some neighbor. Maybe she had even managed somehow to get home. But he found only flood and devastation, the building badly damaged, and the precious new furniture battered and soaked and caked with mud beyond hope of salvage.

As he was about to leave, sick at heart at the destruction of the little home he and Anna had loved so much, he saw an old neighbor poking among the wreckage of the apartment next door, trying to salvage something.

"Pieter de Wilde," called the old man. "Do you come home

soon to stay?"

Pieter put out his hands in a despairing gesture. "Does it look like it?"

"Your wife will put all straight. She's brisk and competent! We all work together," said the old man cheerfully, trying to sort out tools.

"I have had no word of her," said Pieter in a low voice. "No one has."

"Oh, yes," said the old man. "She has been seen by someone here from Middelharnis." He hesitated. "Yes, I'm almost sure it was your wife. Oh, I remember—she was ill. But I think they said she was getting better. Now, where was it? I cannot remember." He took off his cap and scratched his head as if to help him think, but he shook it and said again, "That I cannot remember. But I wish you good luck."

The little encounter, fruitless as it seemed, did give Pieter new hope. He couldn't be sure the old man was right, but at least it was some encouragement.

He could not bear to look further at the little apartment, but he did force himself to go to see what had happened to the store where he kept books. It was badly damaged, and the manager, working there, shook his head when he saw Pieter. "Somehow and sometime we open again," he said. "How and when it is impossible to see just yet. You are safe—you and your family?"

In a few words, Pieter told about Anna, and the man nodded and said, "Go on with your search. I pray God you find her." And once more Pieter set out.

Everywhere he saw men like himself, searching, searching. Questions seemed to be in the very air. Each tried to help the other, and everyone rejoiced when a good answer came, and someone, long sought, was found.

More than once he was told of a young woman who might be Anna; several had seen a young girl who might be Lisa. But though Pieter was alert to follow up each clue, the search ended in disappointment.

When a woman told him one day that she had seen two girls together who answered his description, he shook his head. "That could not be possible," he said, and he walked away. But then the thought struck him that nothing was impossible in these unpredictable days, and he quickly walked back to ask further details.

She had seen the two girls brought to the rescue center at Westmaas in a helicopter, the woman told him. One was dressed as he had described, and—she hesitated here— seemed ill. The other was a pretty, blue-eyed girl with braids wound round her head.

Pieter listened eagerly—this might be right. The description fit. It must be Anna and Lisa! How a helicopter had rescued them, how they had come together, he had not the slightest idea. He only knew that there was hope, but that Anna surely needed him.

His eager questions fairly poured out, but the woman had little more information to give. She had been transferred from Westmaas soon afterward, but she believed—again she hesitated—the young woman had perhaps not been well enough to move. There were Red Cross nurses, she added quickly—very kind, very competent.

Westmaas was a good distance off, and Pieter must have faster transportation than his boat. It seemed that many people knew of his long search and of his valiant work in rescuing others. Inquiries were promptly made, and soon he was offered a place in a motor launch going that way.

The journey to Westmaas seemed very long, and Pieter

was the first one out of the boat, his long legs speedily
covering the distance to the rescue center. A woman came
to him at once—the same woman who had welcomed and
helped Lisa.

"You are looking for someone, I see," she said, and listened
intently to his swiftly told story and eager questions.

But though her eyes were full of sympathy, she had to
shake her head. "I remember them well. They were brought
here by helicopter, it is true, and oh, how I wish I could tell
you where they are now! The young girl was so anxious about
her aunt, so anxious to get some word home—but there was
no way. The pilots had finished their work there and had to
go on where they were needed. The lady—your wife—the
nurses felt should be taken to some place where she could
have better care. All this is just emergency, as you see. Folks
have been brought from many places and taken to many
places from here, and I just don't know where to tell you to
look next. But then," she added, brightening, "the nurses—
maybe they will know. Though I think there is only one now
who was here at that time."

The nurses wanted very much to be helpful, Pieter could
see that. "But people were taken to so many different places,"
they kept saying. "Wherever they could be cared for, even as
far away as Rotterdam, some of them farther. Surely they will
communicate with you before long."

"That could be weeks yet," said Pieter, "unless word was
brought by some acquaintance who chanced to see them.
Could I perhaps have some sort of list—of possible places
where they might be?"

"I think they would not have moved Vrouw de Wilde any
farther than they absolutely had to," said the woman who had
talked to him first. "Why not try the nearest places?"

Pieter's thin, eager face, his quiet determination, and his very evident gratitude made them all want to help him. When he went away, with many thanks and promises to let them know how he fared in his search, he carried a list in his pocket. Now for the first time, he felt he could work intelligently with good hope of success. No one doubted he would find Lisa, and though the nurses' faces had been sober when they spoke of Anna, Pieter never doubted that he would find her too.

9

The Search Ends

Pieter found it difficult indeed to go at the search with the systematic patience he knew it required. His hopes and expectations were high, now that he had real information. He was the one now who wished for a helicopter. Once or twice, he was fortunate enough to get that kind of transportation; at other times he was thankful for motor launches, fishing boats—anything that would get him on his way.

To one place after another he went, checking each off his list, beginning to fear that Anna had been taken farther away than they had thought.

And then, in the little town of Apeldam, he was sure it was Lisa he saw whisking around a corner. He was walking fast already, but now he quickened his long strides and turned the corner himself just in time to see his niece going into a trim little brick hospital. In another moment he was in the building himself, hurrying down the corridor after her, calling softly, "Lisa!"

Lisa stopped and turned slowly, as if she couldn't believe her own ears. Then she rushed toward him, holding out her hands, and he caught them and held them fast. "Where's Anna? Is she—all right?" he asked swiftly.

"She's here! She's going to be all right! Oh, Uncle Pieter!" Lisa had not wept during all the long, difficult days, but now her eyes brimmed over. She turned quickly away, leaned her arm against the wall, put her head down on it, and began to sob as if she could never stop.

Uncle Pieter stood looking compassionately, yet helplessly down at her for a moment. Then he put his hands on her shoulders and turned her gently around. "Why, Lisa," he said. "We aren't going to have another flood, are we, just when we're shoveling our way out of the first one?"

Lisa shook her head, found her handkerchief, and dried her eyes. She managed to laugh a little shakily. "I'm all right now. I don't know what made me act like that. I haven't cried a tear so far. It's just—"

"Don't I know!" said Uncle Pieter fervently, patting her shoulder. "I felt about the same way when I saw you. After all the—well, never mind that now. Let's find Anna. We'll forget all that hard part and just be thankful, won't we?"

"You bet!" said Lisa, but her long sigh was eloquent.

"You'd better go first," Uncle Pieter said, "and tell her I'm here."

Lisa hurried ahead and went into the room first, but Pieter

was at the door, unable to wait. When he saw Anna, white
and wan but sitting up in bed, he was in the room and beside
her in a flash, holding her as if he could never let her go.

And Anna, her head against his shoulder, there in the
ward of a strange hospital, felt as if she had come home
again. "Oh, Pieter! Oh, Pieter!" was all she could say at first,
but there was such relief and happiness in her voice that it
satisfied her husband, though tears were rolling down her
cheeks. Pieter had to struggle hard, indeed, to keep tears back
himself.

"Pieter—our baby we were going to have—we lost it," she
managed to whisper.

Pieter's arms tightened around her. "But I have you," he
said huskily. "I have you, my little Anna."

Perhaps it was as well that a nurse came in just then with
soup for the patients. "So now he found you! Good!" she
exclaimed. "The baby," she added compassionately, "we are so
sorry about that. But there will be others." She gave Pieter a
warm smile and plumped up Anna's pillows. "This is no time
to cry—not for a girl who has been as brave as this one. Eat
some soup now. You'll all feel better." And she gave Pieter a
bowl too before she hurried away.

There was so much to tell that they hardly knew where
to begin. It all came out in bursts of questions and answers.
Pieter wanted to know how Rex had come to have the
kerchief on his collar, if she had been in the windmill room at
all. Indeed, he wanted to know everything.

"It was Rex who saved her, really," Lisa said.

"Rex and Lisa," said Anna, looking proudly at her niece.
Little by little the story came out—how the waves had carried
her around the end of the barn out of sight, how she had

managed to swim and keep afloat until she could get hold
of a couple of boards torn from something, cling to them,
and rest a little, drifting—swimming—tossed around by the
waves. She said, "I was about worn out when who should
come swimming up beside me but Rex. I could hold to him
with one hand, and he pulled me along. Somehow he got
me over to the old windmill, and I managed to get in the
window, and that's about the last I remember until I woke
up with some nurses in charge and Lisa came in, looking
anxious, and then—well, pretty soon I began to get better,
and we tried to think of all kinds of ways to get word to you."

Lisa added a few words, chiefly about how helpful
everyone had been, of Tante Anna's courage, and of the
kindness of the family with whom she was staying. "They've
crowded themselves into just a little space to make room
for as many of us as possible," she said. "But everybody's
good-natured, and we manage pretty well. The only thing is, I
just couldn't get a message home, and I had to stay with Tante
Anna and—"

"Lisa has certainly been a good soldier," said her aunt
feelingly. "What I'd have done without her, I don't know. I
think she came just at the right time."

"But now how about word home?" Lisa said anxiously.
"You'll want to stay here, Uncle Pieter, of course."

"You bet I will!" said her uncle. "I don't leave this girl
again. The store can't be opened for a while yet, anyway. But
there's plenty I can find to do here, and I'll stay until Anna
can come with me."

He didn't tell his wife that their own little apartment was
all but destroyed, and he didn't know where they would go at

first. Time enough to break that news and try to make plans
when she was a little stronger.

"I was thinking," Lisa said. "I'd better try to get home now.
The folks—well, you know how worried they are. And I can
take word of Tante Anna, too."

"But so many were evacuated. What if your folks are still
away? And do you think you can make it alone?" her uncle
asked somewhat anxiously. "You're not used to—"

"She'll make it," said Tante Anna confidently, and a smile
of complete understanding passed between the two. "Anyone
who bought Lisa for a little nitwit would have a bad bargain."

"And if my folks aren't there, I'll stay at the schoolhouse
or somewhere, and try to find out where they are. But I
think they'll be there," Lisa said. Father and Mother would
manage to get home the first possible moment, she knew
that. Perhaps they had stayed in Kuyfoort all through the
emergency.

Now that Uncle Pieter was here to look after Tante Anna
until she could travel, Lisa could hardly wait to get home.
"How about the boat you came on? Is it going back that
way?" she asked.

"Starting back this afternoon, I believe," he answered.
"And it will get you part of the way home, at least. I'll make
arrangements for you to go with them."

Lisa, who had never gone more than half a dozen miles
from Kuyfoort alone in all her life, did feel some qualms as
she stood at the rail waving goodbye to Uncle Pieter. She
didn't know that her uncle had made it his business to tell
the whole story to the captain. She only knew that everyone
seemed eager to help her and to speed her on her way.

By motor launch, by fishing sloop, even by rowboat she went, and to her great joy the last lap of the journey was made in the sailboat of Gerrit Stuyver, who gave her news of her own people, of his sister Martje, now home at last, and of her own special friend, Paula.

"Your folks did go away for a little while, but they're home again now. We are lucky—very, very lucky," Gerrit said soberly. "Our farms are ruined for the time being, it is true, but we will bring them back. The Netherlands has done that before, more than once, and we'll do it again. And our families are all safe, now that we have good news of you and your aunt."

Lisa nodded, thinking of the anxious days when she had wondered if they would ever have Tante Anna safe again. Gerrit, seeing her serious face, smiled.

"I want to see your folks' faces when they catch sight of you," he said. "There will be joy, I promise you. They haven't said much, but they've been anxious."

Lisa herself felt she could hardly wait to see those dear faces. When Gerrit brought his boat down the canal that edged the van Rossem farm and she looked at the desolation all about her, she could hardly keep the tears back. It didn't look much like home. But then she saw something that did— clean, starched curtains behind shining panes in the upstairs windows.

Those shining window panes, the brave starched curtains, gave Lisa a lift of the heart, for they told her in words of their own that Mother was there, taking up the work just where she found it, starting to make things right and comfortable again.

Before Gerrit could tie up his boat, she was out of it,

hurrying through the mud and into the house, calling eagerly, "Mother! Oma! Everybody! I'm here! I'm home!"

"Lisa! Lisa!" came an answering cry of surprise and joy and welcome. Mother was halfway down the stairs as Lisa rushed upward. "My Lisa! My Lisa!" her mother cried. She threw both plump arms around the girl and held her tightly. "Where have you been, my child? What all has happened to you? Never mind, you're safe home! You're safe! You're home!"

They clung together there on the stairway, half laughing, half crying, until Oma called out from the head of the stairs, "Hurry up here! I want to get my hands on that Lisa girl too!"

Gerrit had dashed out to the barn to get Father and the boys, and Rex came flying in ahead of them all, barking his enthusiastic welcome while Gerrit stood by, watching the joyful reunion, well pleased at having some part in it.

Lisa was hugged and exclaimed over and questioned and hugged again, and her story was heard with exclamations of wonder and relief and gladness.

"So you were the one who got there before us and found Tante Anna!" exclaimed Dirk. "She really had been there in the mill, then."

"Oh, yes, she was! But it was Rex, really," said Lisa, patting the dog.

"Yes, Rex did his best to tell us, too," said Dirk, and it was Lisa's turn to listen in wonder as he told his part of the story.

"Good thing you got there right when you did, Lisa," commented Father.

"And you actually had a ride in a helicopter!" said Dirk, somewhat enviously.

"You'll have your turn, Dirk," said Klaas, giving him a

friendly shove. "Remember my wish? Lisa's wish for an adventure certainly came true. You'll see—some of the other wishes will, too, and you can be the first passenger in my helicopter."

As usual, Klaas managed to bring a laugh, but Dirk couldn't help saying, "Hope my wish will come true." He glanced at his father out of the corner of his eye.

Father didn't seem to hear him. "Didn't I wish for the best farm around Kuyfoort, or something like that?" he said, and in spite of himself, he sighed. "It's going to take a long time to make that come true—if ever," he added, half under his breath.

"Well, anyway," said Mother cheerfully, "they're going to inspect our house before very long now, and maybe they'll let us come home to live. We're staying at the schoolhouse yet, Lisa."

Lisa nodded. She had seen so much of that kind of living in the past weeks that it seemed quite natural. "But you've done wonders here," she said. "It looks—it looks like home— almost." For Mother had managed to bring cleanliness and some air of comfort to the upstairs rooms, though the ground floor was still inches deep in mud and sand.

"The Stuyvers came over and helped," said Mother, smiling at Gerrit.

"You helped us, too," Gerrit returned.

"Yes, that's the way we're doing now—each helping the others, wherever it's safe to get into the houses and work."

"And I'd better be going home with my news," said Gerrit, laughing, "or it won't be safe for me to get into our house. The girls will kill me. They'll be wanting to see Lisa, first chance."

"Well, thank you for bringing our girl home," said Mother.

"Klaas did as much for us, though in a different way," said Gerrit, and gave his friend a wink as he went away.

His going didn't check the brisk talk. There was so much to tell, so much to ask. Their neighbors, the Klupts, were still away—would be evacuated for some time with those small children and their house badly damaged. The same was true of many of the other neighbors. But the work of cleaning went briskly forward.

"Women volunteers have come in from other towns and villages—even college girls from as far away as The Hague. And they can work, in spite of their lipstick and manicures," said Oma, with somewhat surprised approval.

"We call all these women with mops and scrub brushes the Flying Squadrons," Klaas grinned. "I guess they've got them all over the flooded places."

"Yes, the houses we are repairing and cleaning up," said Father soberly, "and rebuilding, where necessary. But the land—that will be a more difficult matter. That will not go so fast."

He paused and looked out of the window, and Lisa, following his gaze, saw that the shining windows framed a forlorn sight. The new barn was badly damaged, and there was rubbish scattered over the fields—wood and stones and pieces of machinery, even a wagon up-ended and sunk deep in the mud. The land was covered with gray silt. And, strangest sight of all, onions clung to bushes and trees as if they had grown there.

"How did the onions get there?" Lisa asked.

"Washed from their storage places," said Father. "Potatoes, too—the part of the crop we had been saving to sell later."

"But at least we had some stored for our own use in the attic," said Mother.

Her voice was cheerful, but as Lisa looked out, her heart sank. She didn't see how even as good a farmer as Father could ever transform that gray, muddy waste into a good farm again. "How can you ever get it—" she began, and then stopped, unwilling even to frame the question.

"You wonder how we can ever get it going again," said her father, nodding. "To tell the truth, I guess that question has come to all of us. We'll do it somehow, but I'll admit I don't see my way very clear. All the rubbish must first be cleared away—the rocks and timbers and broken pieces of machinery and everything—"

"We'll get all that junk the flood left cleared out when things have had a chance to dry a little," said Klaas. "What bothers me is how we'll get the soil fit to use."

"Gypsum," said Dirk unexpectedly, for in reading the scientific magazines he loves, he had picked up an astonishing bit of incidental information.

"What do you know about gypsum?" asked his father quizzically, but the boy's interest in the soil pleased him, and he listened and nodded with a look of half-surprised approval as Dirk gave a ready explanation of how gypsum could counteract salt and sweeten the soil once more.

"Yes, it's been done here before now," Father agreed, "but it's a long process and slow—spreading gypsum all over the land. And just where the gypsum is to come from, I don't quite know. Our cattle are all gone, so there will be no milk checks from the cheese factory. Our onions and potatoes are gone. I had counted on those. It may be I must find other work to do for a time. Dike workers are needed everywhere now, with all the old dikes to mend and new ones to build."

A feeling of dismay came over Lisa. She couldn't imagine her father anywhere but on the farm, and she was sure that was exactly where he wanted to be. "Oh, I know you'll make it somehow, Father," she said impulsively. "Right here."

"Well, we'll try our best. There is plenty to do here, if we can find the means to do it."

"You'll do it," said Oma confidently. "I've seen you at work before."

Her son-in-law looked heartened and gratified, but he said, "Much of our machinery is broken—all of it rusted with salt water. We are working to try to get that in some kind of shape, though what we can use to plow with and so forth is something else again."

"We've got Dapple," Klaas reminded him,

"Yes, and we're thankful for that. Of course Dapple is a young horse—high-spirited and not steady like the old ones. But he is a horse, at least," Father said, and his voice had its old hopeful ring. "We'll begin again. We'll make it!"

Once more Dirk surprised him, this time by saying, "Well, let's get back to that machinery." This was one farm chore he found interesting, and he would have been both pleased and surprised to know how favorably his work had impressed his father.

During the talk an idea had come to him—an idea that seemed so practical he didn't see how anyone could object to it. And yet it would work right in with his own cherished plans. He was so excited over it that he wanted to tell it right away, but some feeling of caution told him it would be better to talk it over with Klaas first.

He resolved to do that, the very first chance he had. And from the bottom of his heart, he hoped he could get permission to carry his idea through.

10

A New Start

Much as Lisa longed to stay at home, even to sleep in that once-despised cupboard bed off Mother and Father's room, there was fun and excitement in going to the schoolhouse again. She found it much more comfortable now, equipped with cots and tables.

In one room, a relief center had been set up for the distribution of clothing, food, and other supplies contributed by many countries, including their own. Vrouw van Rossem was active in this work, and as she showed Lisa the warm, sturdy clothing and stores of food and bedding, she said proudly, "And no one here has asked for more than he actually needed—less, in fact. One old man got a good overcoat, and then he found his own, sodden by the flood. He dried it out and brought the other one back, and we couldn't make him keep it."

Lisa felt a little glow of pride that she belonged to such folks—in sore need and accepting the most necessary help thankfully, but standing sturdily on their own feet as far as possible.

Somewhat to her embarrassment, the story of her rescue of Tante Anna had been spread by Gerrit, and she found herself for a time in unfamiliar limelight. But to her relief, it didn't last long, for there were many other stories of courage and quick action waiting to be told. One thing she was sure of—everyone was as glad to have her safely home as she was to be there.

The big question in everybody's mind now seemed to be which houses would be pronounced safe by the inspectors and when permission would be given to move back. Everyone was eager to get home, to begin the work of putting things in shape once more.

The men talked of farm problems, of new dikes, and of how best to start repairs on shattered farm and village buildings. The women, mending and serving as they talked, tried to plan ways of getting along with what they could salvage.

"Our beds," said one of them. "I don't know when we'll ever get them dried out. And so many of our dishes broken—washed right off the shelves. Chairs and tables smashed, floors thick with mud."

There was a moment's silence, and a little sigh of discouragement went around the group. Then Vrouw van Rossem spoke up, with a twinkle in her eye. "I remember once when Dirk was very small and he was trying to move a good-sized table. I said to him, 'You can't move that, boy. It's as big as you are.' And he said, 'Yes I can. I'm as big as it is.' This job we have on our hands is big, but let's hope we're as big as the job."

There was a lift of the heads, ready nods, and laughter. Paula's mother voiced the thought of many there when she said, "The flood didn't beat us, and the aftermath isn't going to either. And now maybe we all ought to get some sleep so we'll be big enough for those jobs waiting for us tomorrow."

Lisa, lying wide awake on a cot near her mother, was thinking of the wish she had had for a room of her own. All that seemed so long ago! Now if they could just get into their own home again, how contented she would feel! But when would that be? And Father, she knew, was worried. She couldn't bear the thought of his leaving his beloved farm for other work, but what could he or any of the men do with that desolate gray land?

She moved restlessly, and Mother's voice near her spoke very softly. "Go to sleep, my Lisa. Tomorrow's a new day." She reached over to pull the blanket up around the girl's shoulders. "We'll just do each job as it comes to hand, and we'll find a way to plan for the future."

Lisa snuggled down with a relaxed little sigh. Mother didn't act troubled. What that plan for the future could be, Lisa didn't see, but if anyone could find it, Mother and Father could. And tonight, at least, she could say something she had been longing for many nights to say. It was nothing more than a murmured, "Good night, Mother," as she drifted off to sleep.

Dirk, too, was wide awake, trying to think his plan out, to hit on the very best way to broach it to Father. He had hoped very much to talk it over with Klaas, but the crowded schoolroom offered no opportunity to discuss a private matter. His thoughts went round and round until at last, right in the midst of his planning, he fell asleep.

But as the two boys worked together in the machine shed the next morning, trying to polish the rust and salt-water erosion off the plow, Dirk said, somewhat diffidently, "I've thought of a way maybe I can get a start on that engineering business."

Klaas' face was sober. He had been thinking longingly of the home he wanted to make for Martje. Right now it looked a long way off. This seemed a queer time for Dirk to be mentioning such ambitions. "Right now, do you mean?" he asked in surprise. "When there's so much to be done here?"

Dirk flushed a little, for his brother's good opinion was important to him. "Well, Klaas, Father was right when he said dike workers are needed everywhere. Maybe I could do some of that. I know quite a bit now about helping with mends."

"So you want to start out as an engineer's assistant," said Klaas quizzically.

"No, of course not," Dirk returned indignantly. "I've got *some* sense. But, Klaas, even placing stones and sandbags and all that, I've learned about things. I've learned some things already. And when I was helping on the dikes, I heard talk about wonderful new dikes they're planning for far into the future, better than we've ever had—stronger and to take in more land. I want to have a hand in helping with all that. And then," he added, "I'd be earning some money that would help out here at home right now when it's needed."

He was sure this would be a telling argument, and he could see that it made a favorable impression. His rush of earnest words had its effect too. Klaas nodded and said soberly, "That is true, of course; the money would come in handy. I can see there's sense in your idea. And in time, I suppose we'll catch up with the work here. But what about school? If you're going to study engineering, you've got to get in plenty of preparatory work."

"I know that," said Dirk. "But I could do part-time work on the dikes. There will be plenty of things a big strong fellow like me, going on fifteen, can do."

Klaas nodded again. "It may be your plan is not such a bad one. But I'll tell you what I'd do. I wouldn't say anything about this for a little while. Father's got so much on his mind, and there is so much to be done here. Let's get the machinery in as good order as we can, first—you are handy at that—and see how things go for a bit. Then if you want to talk to Father, I'll back you up."

This wasn't quite the way Dirk wanted it. He was always impatient to act on a new idea. But he could see there was good common sense in Klaas' advice, and he agreed to follow it.

He had been glad of the opportunity to talk alone to this brother, but now Klaas said, "We've got this about as good as we can get it. Wonder what Father'd like to have us tackle next. We'd better go and find out. I heard him hammering away in the barn a little while ago."

There was no sound of hammering now. Father was standing at the battered barn entrance talking to two strangers, and there was a disturbed look on his face. The boys hastened their steps, for it looked as though new trouble had come up.

"When you plow, be careful not to go too deep," one of the men was saying. "So as to turn under as little salt as possible."

"Guess the best thing you can do is to plant summer barley here," said the other. "That's a salt-resistant crop, and you don't have to keep cultivating it—digging up the ground."

"Summer barley!" echoed Father. "There's no money in

that. Onions and potatoes, sugar beets—those are our crops here."

The men shook their heads. "Take two or three years, anyway, I'm afraid, before you can expect a normal harvest of those crops," one of them said. "Flax may do all right, alfalfa, and a few other things. Got to spread gypsum first of all."

"And in the meantime, what do we live on?" Father asked dryly. "And where do we get the gypsum?"

"Government will help with all that. Didn't we tell you we were from the Agriculture Department?"

There was relief in Father's face now. "Yes, you did, that's right. But I thought the government was just going to tell us what we had to do. I didn't know it was going to help us."

"We're going to help every farmer who is willing to cooperate. Some few are determined to stick to onion raising and so forth, and they don't get flood damage. These your boys here? Looks as if you've got good help."

"I'll need it," said Father, but his voice was full of optimism now as they discussed plans for the future. Where sand had been carried in, bulldozers would take it out; drainage canals would be cleared of sand and mud and roads put back in shape. The government was prepared to help all it could, but every farmer had his work cut out for him.

* * *

The glad day came at last when permission was granted to move back home. No one seemed to mind the crowding in the small upstairs rooms or the monotonous diet of hearty pea soup or pork and cabbage and potatoes cooked in a big pot on the little bedroom stove.

Mother and Oma and Lisa managed the scrubbing and

the backbreaking washings necessary under makeshift conditions, but they needed help in moving furniture and carrying things out into the sunshine to dry, and with these chores Dirk helped, though most of his time was spent on farm work.

Impatient as he was to be off on the dikes, Dirk could see that Klaas' advice was good. There was a great deal of work at home. The sacks of gypsum came, and together Dirk and his father and Klaas worked, each of them carrying a sack, painstakingly walking back and forth the length of the farm. Father scattered the soil-saving chemical evenly, with wide sweeps of his arm. Klaas soon learned to do almost as well. Dirk, trying his best, was encouraged to get a nod and a, "Pretty well, boy. You're getting the hang of it," from his father.

One day, as Dirk worked, he was startled by the clang of a bell and the sight of a fire engine chugging down the road toward their farm. He looked in quick alarm at the house. "All we need is a fire!" he said aloud.

But there was no fire, and now he saw Mother come to the door, looking as surprised as he had felt, even while she greeted the men with her usual politeness.

Dirk left his bag and hurried across the field. So many things were happening these days. He'd better find out what was the matter. But as he came near the house, he saw Mother's look of alarm change to one of pleasure and heard her say, "Good! Good! That will help us indeed! Come, Dirk," she called, catching sight of her son. "Come and see. Something very good and very unexpected is going to happen. This engine here comes from up north to hose down our walls."

"It's a service quite a few of us are volunteering," said the man in charge. He nodded at Dirk with a look of approval, for he could see that the boy was looking at his fire engine with the intelligent interest it deserved. "You like engines," he said with a smile.

"Yes, *sir*," replied Dirk, and his mother nodded.

"We have here a boy who loves engines and anything to do with engineering but is patient to stay on the farm while he is needed here to help," she said.

Dirk felt a glow of pleased surprise. He hadn't thought anyone but Klaas knew, and here Mother seemed to understand all about it. Could it be possible that Father did, too, he suddenly wondered. But that seemed most unlikely.

"Have to do the job that's nearest first," agreed the man. "That's right. I have a feeling you'll get where you want to get, boy. You look like a worker. Now you'll like to watch this job we do."

It seemed like magic to Dirk as the big hoses washed mud off walls and then sprayed water on the floor until the beautiful tiles emerged once more.

"All clean," said Mother, with a deep, happy sigh, "and not much wetter than before."

"Another machine comes tomorrow and pumps hot air all through the rooms and dries things out for you," said the man. "And now we go on to do the same for others."

With many thanks from Mother and Oma, and from Father, who had come up too, the men folded up the hoses, put them back in place, and chugged away over the muddy road, waving as they went.

The truck fitted up to blow hot air into the rooms came the next day, according to promise. "It huffs and it puffs like the wolf in the story of the three little pigs," said Lisa.

When the blower truck was finished, Mother pushed her sleeves up a little higher—as if she could work any harder than she had been doing! "Now we move back downstairs," she said with satisfaction.

Little was said about the badly damaged furniture. Mother and Oma and Lisa, all three, were beaming with pleasure as they went about setting things in order. Everything was carefully sorted out, the usable articles washed and polished, the badly broken ones set aside to be mended if possible, the hopelessly ruined put in a pile to be carted away.

A few things were missing—among them Mother's cherished silver heirloom teapot. "Things have turned up in peculiar places," she said, "but that seems to have disappeared completely. Well, that's not so important, is it, when we have all our family together? I wish the same were true of all our neighbors."

She spoke cheerfully, but Dirk knew that this teapot had been one of her treasures, and he determined that someday he would get her another as nearly like it as possible. He saw plenty of her prized dishes and glassware, as well as some favorite pieces of furniture, in the broken pile to be carted away, and he made up his mind that the day would come when he would replace some of those also.

Outdoors, too, much clearing away was done. "We can't do it all at once," Father said, "but we'll keep right at it."

The work went steadily forward. They were all full of delight when a cow was supplied them. "It is wonderful how the government is helping," said Father. "We are getting some new trees to help replace the ruined orchard, and in a few weeks we start planting—summer barley." He smiled at the mention of the somewhat despised crop.

Indoors, the workers sang as they put the downstairs rooms in homelike order.

"Oh, Mother, doesn't it look *nice*?" exclaimed Lisa, when

the last freshly starched curtain was hung and the rug spread before the tiled fireplace.

And indeed, though the furniture was scanty and many treasures were missing, though the walls were almost bare, everything was spotlessly clean. Thanks to the truck which had pumped hot air through the rooms, the dampness and dank smells were almost gone.

"I think we should have a party," said Oma.

"With so much furniture gone, there's room here to dance," said Mother, smiling. "But what we would offer the guests to eat is something else again."

"In the supplies that were sent to help us, I saw molasses— and some raisins," said Oma. "We could make *roggebrood* and maybe even a cake. I wasn't thinking of a big party." She glanced out of the window and pointed to Klaas, painstakingly guiding the plow so as not to go too deep and trying to keep the frisky young horse going steadily ahead. "I think there is a reason Klaas would like a party."

"Martje, you mean!" said Lisa, with a joyful clap of her hands. "Oh, Mother, couldn't we have a party! But we should wait, shouldn't we," she added, turning suddenly sober, "until Uncle Pieter and Tante Anna can be here?"

There was a short silence. No word had come yet from these absent ones, and Oma voiced the thought of all three when she said, "I would like to know how it goes with those two—if Anna is getting strong again now, and what of Pieter's job, and where they will live."

All these questions had gone through Lisa's mind many times since she got home. The time she had spent with Tante Anna had brought them very close together, and she longed to know of her welfare. "We can't celebrate without them, can we? I think they'll be coming soon now," she said, but her voice faltered as she remembered how very white and thin Tante Anna had looked. "Only, will it seem like a party without our silver teapot?"

"It will seem like a party all right, if only we're all together again," said Mother. "There will be plenty to celebrate then." She nodded with resolute cheerfulness. "Yes, we'll see what we can plan. We'll manage some kind of celebration, you'll see. When Pieter and Anna get back—then we'll have our party."

Lisa fervently hoped that that would be soon.

11

Homecoming Party

Dirk, hard at work chopping down a dead apple tree one sunny spring afternoon, looked up to see his sister Lisa coming swiftly across the fields toward him, Rex trotting along beside her.

"News! News!" she called out. "Uncle Pieter and Tante Anna—they're coming—they're coming this Saturday evening! That's tomorrow! Oh, Dirk!" Her face was one broad smile as she came up, and for a moment they just stood beaming at each other.

This was not the first word that had come. They knew the two were back in Middelharnis—not in their own apartment as yet, but in a comfortable-enough boardinghouse, and that

Uncle Pieter was helping to get the store back to something like normal. And now came the letter announcing the long hoped-for visit.

"Wonder how it will look to them," Lisa said, gazing about her. Where a flourishing little orchard had blossomed last spring, dead trees stood now. The fields no longer held neat rows of onions, and Father's prized herd was missing from the pasture.

But two or three lambs frisked about their elders in the sunshine, and a black and white cow looked over the half door of the barn, apparently keeping an eye on the little flock of yellow chicks peeping, scrambling, and scratching about after their mothers. Some of the dead trees had already been cut down, and healthy ones planted, and barley, beginning to thrust its way through the still-salty earth, gave a look of spring green to the fields.

"Oh, Dirk! It's spring! Things are really beginning to look all right again, aren't they?"

Dirk, too, looked about him, noting the dead shade trees along the canal and the battered farm buildings, still far from their former neat, well-painted state. Salty grime clung to the red bricks of the house, though Mother had washed it as far as her arms could reach and had scrubbed the trunks of the few tall shade trees, some of which they hoped would live. "We're getting things in shape again," he said stoutly. "It's going to look a lot better to Uncle Pieter and Tante Anna than it did the last time they saw it."

"Dirk, it hardly seems possible that only a few months ago this was all covered with water as high as the dike—that the water was on level with those boats right up there," said Lisa, turning and pointing to the boats lying at anchor high above their heads in the little harbor beyond the dike. "We're really getting on, aren't we?"

"Yes, we are," said Dirk. In spite of himself, he gave a little sigh. "They're getting on with that new dike up there, too, but I'm not helping."

Any time Dirk had left over from school these days was so badly needed here at home that he knew it was no use even to mention his brave new plan to Father. He had told Lisa about it, though, and she gave him an encouraging pat and said, "Your turn will come, Dirk; you just wait and see," before she hurried back to the house to get at the joyful work of preparing for the party.

"It must all be done so quickly," Mother was saying as she came into the kitchen. "We have no time at all to stretch things a bit or try somehow to find some extras."

"This time it isn't so important what's on the table as who's on the chairs," said Oma. "With bread and cheese, we can make a good party."

"With bread and cheese, and perhaps an apple, any party is good with this crew," said Mother. "But, oh," she added wistfully, "for this very special occasion I would so like to have smoked eel!"

To the great pleasure of everyone, this modest wish of Mother was granted. When the visitors arrived, Uncle Pieter put a package down on the kitchen table. In the excitement of the warm, joyful greetings, in which Rex took an active part, no one noticed it. But when Mother said, a trifle huskily, "And so you bring us our Anna back, safe and sound," Anna pointed to the package on the table.

"Better still, we bring you also smoked eel," she said, and laughed a little shakily, for she felt if she didn't laugh, she'd burst into tears at the warmth of her welcome.

The others seemed to know how she felt, especially when Rex came to stand close beside her, putting his head against her knee while she gently stroked him. There were chuckles and nods, but right in the midst of it, Oma frankly lifted a corner of her apron and wiped her eyes.

"Time now to get supper on the table," Mother said briskly, knowing that work—especially as pleasant an activity as this—would steady everyone. "I see the Stuyvers coming now. It may be we have a surprise for you," and she put her hand for a moment on Klaas' shoulder. "And with the smoked eel, what a supper it will be! We have also cheese and a canned ham, and Oma found molasses and rye flour to make *roggebrood*. There is even a tin of cookies."

She tied a big apron around her waist and set to work, Lisa and Anna and the Stuyvers all helping. The men and boys took Uncle Pieter out to inspect the flood damage and see what had already been accomplished in bringing things back to normal.

Mother had spoken of a surprise for Uncle Pieter and Tante Anna, but Dirk had a surprise for his mother. When the inspection tour was almost over, he slipped away to the hayloft and smuggled a package hidden there into the house.

The old dining table, battered and flood soaked though it was, had been polished and repolished. Now, covered with Mother's best cloth and set out with what was left of her best blue and white dishes, with a few spring flowers Lisa had brought from the schoolhouse garden, it looked very festive.

"Are you coming with the tea, Lisa?" called her mother, for a good deal of giggling was going on in the kitchen, where Lisa and Dirk were busy.

"Here I am," answered Lisa, and she brought in the big brown earthen teapot.

"Well, the old teapot makes good tea," said her mother, starting to pour, "even if it doesn't look as much like a party as the silver one."

Dirk was coming in the door now. "You like this one

better?" he asked, and with a flourish, he set before her the cherished old silver teapot, polished and shining.

"Why, Dirk!" was all she could say at first. "Why, Dirk! Where on earth did you get it?"

"I didn't get it on earth exactly," grinned Dirk. "I got it off a tree! You didn't know we were growing teapots instead of apples now, did you?" and as the others listened with exclamations of wonder, he told how he had caught a gleam of something high in the tree he was chopping. "So I just climbed up and there it was—your old silver teapot that the flood had hung there. Good thing I spied it, too. It might have been badly scratched and dented if it had come down with the tree."

"Something good was washed up from the flood, you see," said Martje.

"More than one thing," Klaas said, with a smiling, sidewise glance at her.

"Oho!" cried Tante Anna. "Now I think I know the surprise Sister promised us. We are to have a new niece in the family one of these days—is that it?"

Right in front of everyone, Klaas put his arm around Martje's shoulders and gave her a hearty hug. "You bet!" he said. "We're going to work toward a home of our own, aren't we, Martje? And we'll keep at it, no matter how long it takes, won't we?"

And Martje's shining eyes were enough of an answer.

"Do you remember the wishes we made the night of the flood?" Lisa asked eagerly. "We were playing a game of wishes," she explained to the Stuyvers, "and Klaas wouldn't make his wish out loud. He said his big wish was for a helicopter, but I knew well enough it was for you, Martje."

Martje blushed as all the others laughed, and Mother looked quickly from the happy face of her older son to the wistful face of Dirk. Klaas would undoubtedly make his wish come true, even if it took several years; but what of her restless, eager Dirk, who had worked so hard during the flood and was working equally hard now to help get the farm in shape once more?

"I wished for an adventure," Lisa said, somewhat ruefully. "I certainly got my wish a lot faster than I expected, and enough to last me the rest of my life. I wonder if some of the other wishes will come true. Uncle Pieter said that night he had his wish—it was Tante Anna."

"And I still have her. I thank God," said Uncle Pieter, reaching for her hand and holding it tightly.

His wife looked up at him, and her eyes were very bright. Lisa felt a lump in her throat. But then Tante Anna said, with her old gay chuckle, "But I never did get my dishpan! Maybe Dirk can find one on a tree for me someplace." That made them all laugh.

"And I wished that we might always be as well off and happy together as we were that night," said Mother musingly. "I said then that it was a big wish, but I guess I didn't know how big it was. But see now—how much we have come through! We have a long way still to go, but tonight here we all are, and our good friends the Stuyvers with us. I don't believe I have a wish to make tonight." But her eyes went back to Dirk, and in her heart, there was a wish she didn't mention.

"Your wish, Father, was for the best farm around Kuyfoort," Lisa reminded him.

Father laughed a little, shaking his head. "We're working toward it," he said stoutly. "The Stuyvers here are doing the same."

"But you have two boys to help you—I have just one," Heer Stuyver said.

There was a moment's silence, and then Father said thoughtfully, "I don't know. Dirk here has been doing a man's work on the farm, but I noticed he did a man's work on the dike when needed most, too. Did you know the Queen spoke to him?" he asked proudly.

"Oh, Father!" protested Dirk, flushed and embarrassed in spite of his pleasure.

But Father went right on. "Yes, she told him he had the makings of a good engineer, and the Netherlands needs engineers. I used to think farmers were the most important of all, but when I saw the dike workers in action in the emergency, I realized how much we need engineers, too. Klaas and I have been talking things over. I have in Klaas a boy who's a good farmer; I believe I have one in Dirk who could make a good engineer."

In his excitement, Dirk jumped right up at the table. "Do you mean that, Father?" he burst out, and his eyes were shining. "I was thinking maybe I could get work on the dike after school hours—learn all I can that way—and later on—"

His father nodded thoughtfully. "Sounds like a good, sensible plan," he said. "We'll talk it all over later. We can maybe work it out." His voice said plainly that the thing was as good as settled.

Lisa gave a sigh of pleasure. She had almost forgotten the wish she had had for a room of her own. Somehow it didn't seem at all important now. To have a warm, comfortable bed anywhere at home seemed enough for the present, even if it was a cupboard bed off her parents' room.

But Mother was saying, "I believe I do have one little wish, after all. When we get things squared away, one of these days, I'd like to make a little room in the attic for Lisa. She's grown up so much these last weeks; she should have that."

Lisa almost hugged herself in her delight. Instead she gave

Dirk, who was sitting beside her, a hearty nudge with her elbow. "Oh, Dirk," she said, "do you hear our wishes coming true? Did you ever think that stormy night—"

Dirk shook his head. He was almost too happy to speak, and he had to get used to the idea that he could begin to work toward his ambition, and with Father's help and approval.

"No one seems to think a thing about my wish," observed Oma tartly, but her brown eyes were sparkling. "I wished for cotton for my caps for the spring trip to Dordrecht. But my cotton was washed away, and we aren't going to make a spring trip, and —" she paused and finished decidedly, "I don't care one single bit. I may not bother with caps much more. If Klaas is going to a farm of his own, and Dirk is going away to school, my good son here is going to need an extra helper, and I'm applying for the job."

"We'll soon have twenty cows for you to milk," promised Father, joining in the laughter.

"But don't worry, even when I have a place of my own, we'll manage to work together. You'll see," said Klaas.

"We'll manage to work together," said Mother soberly. "Yes, that's what we've been doing—all through the flood—all through the country."

"It's how we're pulling ourselves out of the mud," said Oma. "And now why don't we have a song or two? First let's have that old favorite we sang Sunday in church."

Singing was a favorite form of entertainment with this group, and they all joined heartily as Mother's voice led:

"The floods have lifted up, O Lord,
  The floods have lifted up their voice,
  The floods lift up their waves.

"But the Lord on high is mightier,
 Mightier than the noise of many waters.
 Yea, than the mighty waves of the sea."

Dirk looked at the clean, bare room and the earnest, happy faces of the singers around the lamplit table. They had come a long way since the night of the flood, and now, with the plans for the new dikes, he hoped there would never be such a flood again.

He gave a deep sigh of contentment. It would all take time, but he knew now that he was going to have his part in helping keep his country safe from those "mighty waves of the sea."

More Books from The Good and the Beautiful Library

Trini, The Strawberry Girl
by Johanna Spyri

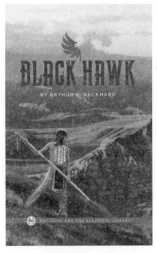

Black Hawk
by Arthur J. Beckhard

The Saracen Steed
by Arthur Anthony Gladd

The Touch of Magic
by Lorena A. Hickok

goodandbeautiful.com